Ignite

USA TODAY BESTSELLING AUTHOR

REBECCA YARROS

www.RebeccaYarros.com

Edited by Karen Grove

Cover design by RBA Designs

Cover art from CJC Photography

ISBN 979-8-9860144-1-8

Manufactured in the United States of America

To Christina.
Running Woman.
For iced coffees, deployment visits,
Cupcakes, phone calls,
saving my sanity,
And yanking me out of my shell.
You are the mom I've always wanted to be.

1

RIVER

*F*uck my life, I was exhausted. Squinting into the sun, I walked out of the Midnight Sun's Hotshot Crew house at 10:45 p.m. I'd never known a more fitting name for a hotshot team in my life. We'd lived here the last seven years—as soon as I'd been accepted to the University of Alaska —but the sunlight situation in late July still caught me off guard from time to time.

Guess my brain always diverted back to Colorado.

"Damn, that was a long one, Riv," Bishop said, swinging his arm over my shoulder and squeezing. He'd done the same thing after every fire we'd ever been on together. I knew he hated that I'd followed him into this life. What the fuck did he think I was going to do? Let my big brother follow in our dad's footsteps and not tag along? Hell no. As soon as I was old enough, I'd applied, worked my ass off through college getting my degree in forestry, and now here we were.

"I'm just glad it's over. It was getting dicey there for a while." I unlocked the doors on my F250 as he ruffled my hair like we were kids again. Strands of the dark, heavy stuff caught in the scruff of my beard as it settled back around my face. Chin-length was as far as I could handle my hair, I had no clue how Bishop managed to keep his down his back.

Our mother is Cheyenne, he always said in explanation.

"It did go to shit," he admitted. "You could always take a cushy job with the forest service. No fires, safe hours, nice scenery…" he said before unlocking the doors to his truck, too.

"Like that's ever going to happen," I said as I tossed my dirt-covered bag into the bed of the truck.

"Yeah, well, I wish it would," he mumbled.

"Gym tomorrow?" I asked, ignoring his jibe. For only being three years older than me, he took his brothering seriously.

"Same as usual," he answered, climbing up into his truck.

I did the same, sliding behind the wheel and shutting the door. A crank of the engine later and I was on the road out of Fair-banks, heading toward my house in Ester. Bishop was a mad man when it came to gym time. *You'd better be able to outrun the fire,* he'd always told me.

So he pushed me like the flames were constantly licking at my heels. Not that I minded the body it gave me—hell, it attracted more than my fair share of female attention. Though I'd defi-nitely sampled the buffet of women up here, my exploits were nothing compared to Bishop's.

We were both the same in one regard, though: we'd never been with one woman longer than six months or so. Bishop tended to leave around that time, and as for me…well, the girls always figured out that they weren't my first priority, which rightfully pissed them off.

As I turned off route three into Ester the sun finally started to set. For God's sake, it was 11 p.m. I missed warm summer nights under the stars in Colorado. Not that Northern Lights weren't amazing...they just weren't the same.

Don't complain about the sunlight. It will be dark nearly all day soon enough.

The lot in front of the Golden Eagle Saloon had an empty parking spot, and I took it, jumping down from the truck once I killed the ignition. I smelled like smoke and ten days of hard firefighting, but I knew she'd lose her shit if I didn't stop by.

Besides, I was itching to see her.

The music was up when I walked into the old-fashioned log cabin saloon. Good crowd for a Saturday night.

"River!" Jessie Ruggles called out from the bar, her skirt a hell of a lot shorter than those long-ass legs of hers called for. Not that I was complaining. "Everybody make it home okay?"

"Yeah, we're intact," I answered. "Have you seen—"

"River!"

I turned toward her voice and was immediately met with a hundred pounds of perfection. She swore it was more. I never believed her.

Avery jumped, and I easily caught her. Her arms wrapped around my neck, one of them cradling the back of my head in that way of hers that always fucking melted me.

"You're okay," she whispered in my neck.

Even in the bar, she smelled fantastic, all apples and warm cinnamon.

"I'm okay, Avery," I promised, my hands splaying on her back. "Everyone is."

She nodded but didn't say anything, just held me a little tighter. I'd come home from countless fires in the years that she'd been my best friend, and this was always how she welcomed me home.

There was nothing better on the planet.

I stood there in the middle of the bar, letting her hold me as long as she needed. Mostly because I could never get enough of her in my arms.

Avery Claire had been my best friend since I was eighteen.

I'd also been silently in love with her for just as long.

Maybe one day she'd be ready to hear it, but I knew that today was not that day. Hell, the next year didn't look promising, either.

Taking in one more deep breath, Avery slid from my grasp, backing up a couple feet once her toes hit the wooden floor of the bar. Then she looked me over, inspecting for anything that might slightly resemble an injury. She tucked her long blonde hair behind her ears and nodded, appeased. Avery was fair everywhere I was dark, her skin pale where mine was deeply tanned by the sun and my mother's Cheyenne heritage. She was tiny where I was broad, curved where I was straight, and those shorts she wore didn't disguise much of her toned legs.

"See, I'm fine," I said with a little grin.

"Promise?" she asked, narrowing those gorgeous blue eyes.

"I smell like smoke and I'm fucking exhausted, but other than that, I'm in one piece. I'm actually headed home, but I figured you were working tonight—"

"And that I'd kick your ass if you didn't tell me you were home."

"I could always text."

"Not the same." Her smile grew until she could have lit the world with how bright it was. "I'm glad you're home."

"Me, too. Did Zeus miss me?"

"Your husky is the neediest, wimpiest dog I've ever met, but yes, he's content and full of treats at your house."

"He's a big baby," I admitted.

"Just like his owner," she teased.

"Avery, were you thinking about getting back to work?" Megan asked from behind the bar in her pack-a-day rasp. She was ageless, frozen somewhere in her fifties. The woman hadn't changed since I got here seven years ago.

"Yeah," Avery called out. "Sorry, I have to go."

"I know. Don't worry. I'll see you tomorrow—"

"Riv!" Adeline came running at me, a tangle of hair and knobby knees.

I caught her easily and squeezed her tight. "Hey, Addy! What are you doing here?"

She pulled back and glanced at Avery. "I was supposed to stay with Stella, but she had to go out of town with her parents."

I nodded and looked over to Avery, who was biting her lip. I knew she hated when she had to bring Addy in—she was only thirteen—but not nearly as much as she hated leaving her home alone with their father.

"Why don't you come spend the night in my guest room?" I asked.

Her eyes flew wide with excitement. "Can I watch *Game of Thrones?*"

"Nope," I answered. "But I think I have every episode of *Arrow.*"

"Okay, I can rock that. Stephen Amell is hot."

"If you say so," I said, grinning at her. Addy never failed to bring a smile to my face.

"Are you sure you don't mind?" Avery asked, her hands wringing.

I wanted to cup her face, brush my thumbs across her cheekbones, and lay a soft kiss to her lips. Instead, I squeezed her hand. "It's no problem. Why don't you come over when you're done? Bunk with Adeline, and we'll go for breakfast in the morning?"

She nodded with a grin. "Yes. I close out at two, and then I'll head over."

I would have said anything to see Avery smile like that—carefree and happy. She was always beautiful, but that smile shot her straight to gorgeous, and I never saw enough of it. "You have a key, so just come on in. Addy, you ready?"

"Yes!"

I laughed at her excitement. "Okay, but don't get too excited. Zeus might want to share your bed, and he's a hog."

"True, but he's nice and warm."

"That he is," I admitted before turning back to her big sister. "See you in the morning?"

She nodded and leaned up on tiptoes to hug me. It was the only way to cross the difference between my six-foot-five frame and her five-foot-six. "Thank you for taking her," she said, holding me tight. "I just couldn't leave her there on her own. He gets so mean at night."

When he's been drinking.

"No problem." I hugged her back and let her slide from my arms.

Then I took Adeline home.

"I love your house," she said as we climbed the steps to the porch.

"It's not as big as yours," I answered, slipping the key into the lock. I'd built the house myself—with Bishop and contracted workers, of course, and I was fond of its traditional log-cabin design, but I knew it wasn't much.

"It feels more like home," she said as I opened the door.

"Umpf!" My breath was knocked out of me as Zeus barreled out the door, tackling me to the ground. All hundred and twenty pounds of him lay on my chest, licking my face as he whined. "Yeah, I missed you, too, buddy," I said, petting his thick fur.

He looked at me with disapproving blue eyes, like I'd had any control over how long the fire had taken, and let me up. I massaged his head a few more times, and he started to forgive me. "Come back when you're done," I told him, and he raced off into the woods. There was something to be said for having ten acres to myself.

I brought two of my fingers to my mouth and then pressed them to the framed picture of my dad that hung just inside the entry. Some rituals had to be kept—and this was definitely one of them. "Made it home, Pop," I said.

"Why did you do that?" Addy asked.

"Because I always tell him I made it when I get home from a fire," I told her, hauling my bag in with me.

"Because he didn't?" she asked.

The innocent question caught me off guard. "That's right. He died with his whole Hotshot team when a fire took our hometown."

She looked up at the photo of my dad in his gear and then back to me. "How long ago was that?"

"Ten years." *Ten years in a couple weeks.*

"That's sad. I'm sorry."

"Thank you. It's hard to lose your parent, huh?"

She nodded. "I don't really remember my mom, though, so..." She shrugged.

"I don't think that makes it any easier. Loss is loss."

She nodded, examining the photo of my father. "He was handsome."

"My mom sure thought so." They had loved each other in a way that told me I'd never settle for less in my own life. "Your stuff is still in the dresser in there," I told Addy as she walked into the living room. This wasn't the first time she'd slept over while Avery worked, and I knew it wouldn't be the last.

"Thanks!" she said, skipping off to the guest room and its seventy-inch television that I bought mostly for her.

As much as I loved Avery, I was a sucker for Adeline.

Zeus cried at the door, and I let him in, then took my bag to the washer. As usual, all of my clothes smelled like smoke. It never really bugged me until I got home. Once I walked into my house, I couldn't wait to get the reek of smoke out of my clothes, my hair, my skin. I tossed them in, dumped detergent, and started the load. Hopefully the smell would come out on the first wash.

It took a long shower to do the same for my body.

After I was clean, I grabbed a beer, turned on the news to catch up on the world, and pulled my laptop onto my lap, checking my social media. Zeus curled up next to me, and I absently pet him while I scrolled.

Drama.

Drama.

Cute baby.

Drama.

Shit, when did he get married?

I'd been gone from Colorado so long that I'd completely lost touch.

After a few minutes I closed the computer, leaving my friends—both from college and home in Colorado—behind as I changed the channel and tuned the world out for a little while.

I'd made it home from another fire. I glanced up at my dad's picture and tipped the beer toward him in salute. Then I took a long pull and leaned my head back on the couch.

"Riv?"

I blinked at the soft voice and raised my head as my beer was pulled from my hand. "Avery?" I asked, my voice husky from sleep.

"Yeah," she said, running her fingers through my hair. "You must have fallen asleep."

"Mmmm." I leaned into her touch. "What time is it?"

"Two fifteen."

I sat up and shook the sleep from my eyes. "No shit?"

"You must be exhausted," she said, snuggling into my side.

I wrapped my arm around her and with the other arm pulled a blanket over her. "I am," I admitted. "I bet you are, too."

"Mmmhmmm," she said, her head finding that perfect spot on my chest as she let out a jaw-cracking yawn.

Do it now. Every time I was in a fire, I swore that I'd come home and tell her how I felt. I knew she didn't want to be in a relationship with anyone—that taking care of her nearly bed-ridden father was all she thought she had time for. That her two jobs and basically raising Adeline on her own were her only priorities…

But I wanted her to know that she was *my* only priority.

So what if it got complicated? Messy? I wasn't going anywhere, and neither was she. We'd find a way to work out whatever got in the way, and even if it took years, I knew she'd be the only one I'd ever want.

Every other failed relationship had already taught me that there was no substitute for Avery Claire.

I took a deep breath and tried to find my proverbial balls. "Hey, Avery?"

She didn't answer.

I moved just enough to see her closed eyes and parted lips, her breath even and deep. She was asleep.

I should have moved her. Instead I leaned my head back on the couch and savored the feeling of falling asleep with her in my arms.

It had only been five minutes when there was a pounding at my door. I sat up with a start, barely catching Avery before she tumbled to the floor. "Who the hell?" I mumbled, glancing at the window. The sun was up already, but that didn't mean much.

"Whoa, it's eight," Avery said, stretching next to me.

I did not look at the way her breasts pressed against the thin material of her tank top.

I did not appreciate her sleepy yawn, where her tongue curled like a little kitten.

I did not immediately picture putting her sleep-warmed body under mine and waking her up fully with an orgasm that would leave that raspy voice screaming my name.

Not at all.

Fuck.

The pounding continued, and I got up and headed for the door, where Zeus was already wagging his tail. I opened the door and he flew out, past where Bishop stood with his lips pressed together. That face was never a good sign.

"Some guard dog you have there," he remarked as he walked in.

"Zeus knew it was you," I said. "Besides, I'm twenty-five years old. Get off my ass. You're only older by three years."

"Yeah," he said, looking up at Dad's picture before striding into the living room. If he didn't rise to that bait, there really was something drastically wrong.

"Hey, Avery," he said into my kitchen where she was putting on coffee.

"Bishop," she said with a smile. "Coffee?"

"That'd be great," he said before turning back to me. "You awake?"

"I answered the door, didn't I?" I crossed my arms over my chest. "We're not supposed to meet up for another two hours, so why are you here?"

His jaw flexed. "I had an early morning phone call."

"From?" Unless it was our father calling from the grave, I couldn't think of a reason good enough to jolt me out of Avery's arms.

"Sebastian Vargas."

"Bash? No fucking way." I shook my head, certain I'd heard him wrong. "Is something wrong at home?" Why the fuck would Bash call? He was on a Hotshot team in California. Hell, he'd left Legacy the same time I did.

Bishop swallowed and flexed his hands. "They're resurrecting the team."

My jaw hit the fucking floor. "I'm sorry. You're going to have to say it again."

He nodded. "Yeah, I made him say it like six times. I honestly didn't believe him until Emerson Kendrick got on the phone."

"Emmy is in on this, too?" Emmy and Bash had both lost their fathers with ours, buried them next to each other on Legacy Mountain.

"I never thought it was possible, but they got the town council to agree on one condition."

"Which is?" Every emotion possible assaulted me, scraping me raw with disbelief, hope, pride, and a touch of wariness. Was resurrecting a team that had been annihilated the best move? Would it do them justice? Was it cursed to suffer the same fate? We'd buried eighteen out of the nineteen of them.

It was everything we'd fought for during the first years after the fire, but as time passed, and we'd been denied over and over... well, it became the impossible.

"It has to be made up primarily of legacies. Blood of the original team."

I stood there, staring at my brother while it sank in. He nodded slowly, like he understood the time it was taking me to process the news of the impossible.

My eyes drifted back to where Avery pulled a steaming mug of coffee from under the Keurig. "Say it," I nearly growled, knowing his next words were about to rip my plans to shreds.

"They can't do it without us. If we want the Legacy Hotshot Crew to be reborn..."

Fuck. My. Life.

"We have to go home."

2
AVERY

He has to what?

The idea of River going anywhere was enough to nauseate me. Maybe I misheard. Maybe Bishop didn't mean it. Maybe that awestruck look on River's face meant something completely different.

The heat from the coffee radiated through the mug, finally burning my hand before I realized I still held it. I rounded the half-wall that separated the kitchen from the living room and handed the cup to River, who looked at me with shocked, deep brown eyes and mumbled his thanks.

"What does he mean?" I asked River.

His strong jaw tensed as he looked back to Bishop. With the stern set of their faces, they'd never looked more like brothers. Their Native American heritage proved dominant, giving them gorgeous, chiseled features, strong noses, high cheek bones, and raven black hair. But although Bishop was an inch or so taller than his little brother, River had at least thirty pounds more muscle on him. Thirty pounds of insanely cut, incredibly hot muscle.

Whoa. No thinking about River like that.

"What exactly *do* you mean?" River asked Bishop.

Every muscle in my body clenched.

"We'd have to move back to Colorado." Bishop's eyes flickered toward me, but mine were on River.

He nodded slowly, like he was working details through his head. That was one thing about River—he never made a decision without thinking it through. "And they have to have us?" he asked.

"They do. They're going to be tight to hit sixty percent as is. Bash said he can't be sure of final numbers yet."

"How long does he have to come up with names?"

A year. Say a year. Nausea hit my stomach hard. I couldn't fathom a life without River around. It was already hell when he was on fires for a few weeks at a time.

"Two weeks."

Okay, now I was going to puke. I must have made some kind of sound, because River's arm came around my shoulders, pulling me into his side where I always thought I'd be. We weren't together or anything, but he was an integral part of what made my world turn.

"Two weeks," he repeated, rubbing the bare skin of my arm with his hand.

"Council only gave him until the ceremony."

"Well, that's just fucking fitting," River growled.

"I don't understand," I said quietly.

River hit me with those impossibly deep eyes, two little lines furrowing between his eyebrows. "Remember I'm headed back to Colorado for the weekend in a couple weeks?"

I nodded.

"That's the deadline they gave Bash," Bishop answered. "They're making this as impossible as they can, even though he's footing the bill for everything. The firehouse is up and everything, it's just missing a crew."

"Damn. I knew he was rich, but not *that* rich." River took a deep breath, and let it out slowly. "Okay, so if we move back, we get to reform the Legacy Crew?"

"That's the plan."

"And if we don't?"

"They fail. There's no mathematical way to do it without the both of us."

River smirked with a sarcastic laugh. "And to think you never wanted me to fight fires."

"Still don't. This isn't an order, River, it's a choice."

"Are you in?" River asked.

"I'm going," Bishop said.

My breath left in a rush. If Bishop was going—

"Then I have to go. There's no way you're doing this on your own. We keep each other alive. Isn't that what you always tell me?"

Pain ripped through me, so intense that I felt the emotion singeing my nerves as though someone had taken a branding iron to my soul.

"Yeah," Bishop said quietly. "Are you sure this is what you want to do?" His eyes passed over me again, like I would make any impact on River's decision. I'd never crossed the line that would give me a say—never given in to the intense chemistry we shared, or the longing I'd always had. It wouldn't have been fair of me, not with the responsibilities I'd taken on.

He deserved better.

River's grip on my shoulder tightened. "It's Dad, Bishop. There's not really a choice. It's his team and our home. If there's a chance to bring Legacy back to life, then I'm not sitting it out."

This was it. He was leaving Alaska. Leaving me.

"Where the hell have you been?" Dad yelled out as Adeline and I walked into our home.

She winced. I gave her a reassuring smile. "I'll take care of him."

"Are you okay?" she asked.

"Yeah," I lied. "Why?"

"You've been on the verge of tears since we left River's house. Did something happen between you two?"

I tucked a strand of blonde hair behind her ear. "No. River and I are fine. It's never been like that between us."

"Well, it should," she said as she walked off.

He was my best friend. It wasn't that I hadn't ever thought of what it would be like—actually being his. I was a woman after all. I already knew nearly every plane and hollow of his body, the way the corners of his eyes crinkled just a little when he full-out grinned. Hell, he'd even starred in some of my most blush-worthy fantasies. But I lived in reality.

"Avery!" Dad yelled from the living room.

A reality with my dad. I steeled my nerves with a deep breath and headed in. "Yes, Dad?"

"Where the hell have you been?" he repeated his earlier question. "You didn't bother to come home after work." He was laid out on the living room couch, wearing yesterday's clothes and reeking of alcohol. Or maybe that was the nearly empty bottle of Jack on the floor next to him. Dishes littered the coffee table, just within his reach.

"We stayed with River last night," I said, stacking the dishes.

"Well, you should have been here, not whoring around with the Maldonado boy."

He didn't even bother to look at me, just went back to watching *Family Feud*. Not that he had any clue what family was. In his mind, that word had only extended to my mother, and with her gone…well, we weren't worth much.

"We're just friends, Dad," I said, taking the dishes back into the kitchen.

"Like hell. Bring me my meds, would you?" he asked, his tone suddenly sweet at the end.

I set the dishes in the sink and turned the warm water on to help loosen the dry, stuck-on food. Then I gripped the edge of the counter and lowered my head, taking in deep breaths.

River was leaving. This was my life. There would be no bright spots of laughter with him, of star-gazing, or stealing the comfort of his arms under the guise of friendship. This was it.

My heart felt like it was being mashed, squeezed until I bled out. The life I led wasn't glamorous, or even really fulfilling. It was duty. Duty to raise Adeline. Duty to take care of Dad.

Duty.

I slammed the pill bottle onto the counter with more force than I'd intended.

Duty.

I twisted off the cap, Dad yelling again from the living room because I was taking too long.

Duty.

And that had seemed fine last night because I had one small thing that I kept for myself: River.

But now I felt like I was staring across the path my life would take...and suddenly the emptiness was overwhelming.

"Avery!" Dad yelled.

"Yeah, Dad. In a second," I answered, knowing that if I didn't, the shouts would only get louder until they turned to yells. Until he started throwing things. And if I put my foot down and made him get up for it...well, shit got broken. Not us—he'd never laid a finger on Adeline or me—just everything we loved, to make his point.

Mom had died in the car crash that had resulted in Dad's fused spine, and we would forever pay for losing her and his never-ending pain and the loss of his job on the force. After all, they'd been on their way to pick us up from a weekend with our grandmother. In Dad's mind, if we'd never been born, she'd still be alive and he'd be whole—still a police officer.

I knew better, whether or not he would ever admit it.

It was the secret between us. He kept it because he'd never willingly expose himself to the consequences of his actions. I kept it because he was Addy's guardian, and the minute I opened my mouth, he'd kick me out of her life, and then what would happen to her? Even if I reported him for neglect, there was no guarantee she'd end up with me.

I rinsed the dishes and put them into the dishwasher, then grabbed Dad's pain meds from the top of the cabinet, where I'd chosen to hide them for the week. Moving them around ensured that he never took more than he was allotted.

I grabbed a bottle of water from the refrigerator and carried the pills to him.

"It's about time," he grumbled and cried out as he sat up on the couch. He swallowed the pills and some of the water, then scratched his hand across his unshaven beard. I'd given up trying to get him to shave years ago. "You think about cleaning this place up?" He motioned around the general dishevel of the living room.

"Maybe later," I answered. "I need to run into the office for a few minutes."

"At the *paper?*" he sneered.

"Yes, at the paper. Where I have a job." *So I can keep the lights on.*

He laughed. "That's not a job. Jobs make real money. Why don't you quit that one and take up more shifts at the bar? Pretty girl like you can make good tips."

I did make good tips. Enough to save up almost a full semester's tuition for Adeline. Five more years and maybe I could get her through college without the loans I'd taken out for my journalism degree. But that degree had also led me to River, which was worth every cent of the debt I'd accrued.

"Okay, well, if that's it, then I have stuff I need to get done."

He turned the channel. "Get me clean clothes and make me breakfast."

I bit the insides of my cheeks and something in me snapped. "Say please."

"I'm sorry?" he asked, finally looking at me, his eyes drug-hazed but wide.

"Say please," I repeated.

"Why should I?" he snapped like a petulant toddler.

The pain of River's inevitable loss morphed into red-hot anger. "Because I haven't changed from work yet. Because I'm holding down two jobs to keep the taxes paid, utilities on, and everything Adeline needs. Because River is moving back to Colorado and this is my life, so I need you to be a little understanding today, Dad, okay?"

"Losing your boyfriend, huh?" he asked, turning his attention back to the television. I had the overwhelming urge to throw that goddamned remote through the screen.

"He's not my boyfriend."

"Then why do you care so much? Let him move on, find a woman who can take care of him. Be happy that he's getting the hell out of here, because we never will."

I never will.

"Nice. Really supportive."

"You're right," he said with a little shrug.

My chest lightened just a little, like the man I'd loved more than life was peeking through the clouds that had covered him the last eleven years. "Oh?"

"This is your life. You earned it. Now get my clothes, these smell."

"Shower once in a while," I threw over my shoulder as I walked away from him and the smell of funk that had become the norm of that room since he'd decided he was done walking to bed.

"Watch your mouth!" he yelled.

I made my way up the stairs and into my bedroom where I flung myself onto the bed and stared up at the ceiling.

Put him in a home.

Move out and leave.

You're an adult now; you don't have to stay.

The words of advice all of my friends had given raced through my head as I lay there. But those friends had all moved on. They'd gone to warmer climates, bigger cities. They weren't responsible for the care of their parents.

Family has a way of pushing us to our limit...but we just keep moving the limits for them. River's voice overpowered every other thought. He'd always understood why I stayed when everyone else left.

I looked over at the picture of us from last summer on the water. His arms were around me, his chin resting on my head as we both grinned at the camera. His chest was bare, the tribal tattoos stretching across his chest and bringing more attention to the definition of his muscles, the tight, honed lines he worked so hard to keep perfect.

As he reminded me constantly—it wasn't vanity but the way he stayed alive and one step ahead of the fires he fought.

Then again, I'd never seen him argue when he turned the head of every woman within fifty miles. He'd just smile back, wink, and I knew their panties would happily drop to his bedroom floor.

Not that I was allowed to be jealous. For starters, we weren't together. He could sleep with every woman in Fairbanks and I wouldn't get to say a damn thing. Not that any of them were good enough for him. But I also had a part of him that none of them ever would. Our friendship had outlasted every failed relationship on both our parts. If there was a constant for us, it was each other.

How the hell was that going to work with him in Colorado?

Would he move, find a hometown girl?

Would I get a wedding invite? A birth announcement? Would his world widen into something beautiful while mine stayed stagnant here—without him?

It should, I told myself. River deserved everything. A beautiful, kind wife who would give him little boys with his eyes and little girls with his hair and courage.

How was I going to put on a brave face while he prepared to move? I couldn't make him choose—and it wasn't like I had much to offer.

Here, River. You have the world at your fingertips and every woman in the country to choose from, but pick me. I come complete with a little sister to raise and an invalid, drunk father. Aren't I a bargain?

I pulled my pillow into my chest, like it could fill the emptiness threatening to make me implode, simply crumple into myself until there was nothing left.

My phone rang with his ringtone and I swiped to answer.

"Hey, Riv."

"Hey, Ava. You ran out of here pretty fast this morning."

Silence stretched along the line while I composed my answer. It wasn't fair to unload on him, to take all of my insecurities, all the responsibilities in my life, and thrust them on him. "Yeah, I just had a lot to do, and it sounded like you did, too."

"My head is kind of swimming, honestly."

My teeth sank into my lower lip. "I bet."

"I never thought they'd restart the team," he said quietly. I knew what it meant to him, his father's literal legacy.

I wanted to talk to him. I did. I just didn't know how to bury my misery deep enough to not lay it on him. He didn't need my selfish shit on top of everything else.

"I totally get that. But hey, can we talk later? I have to run by the office." I congratulated myself on not letting my voice crack.

"Yeah, of course. Avery, are you okay?" he asked.

My eyes slid shut as a sweet pressure settled in my chest at his concern. He always made me feel precious, protected. In a world where I spent almost every waking moment taking care of everyone else, he was the only one who cared for me.

And now it was my turn to take care of him.

"Absolutely. I'm fine."

The lie was sour on my tongue and nauseated me the moment it left my mouth. This was anything but fine. The thought of losing him hurt so deeply that I was almost numb with shock, afraid to look at the damage or see the hemorrhage.

But he could never know that.

3

RIVER

*C*ould this day get any fucking worse?

The realtor told me the state of the housing market up here meant I was going to lose money when I sold my house, I'd just had to tell Midnight Sun that I needed to give notice, and Avery was fucking *avoiding* me.

Even when I'd been in my most serious relationship, she'd never pulled that shit. It had been two days since she'd told me she was "absolutely fine" and ran off to work.

In those two days I'd signed a listing agreement with a date to be determined, arranged to stay an extra day in Legacy for house-hunting, and contacted a moving company about getting my crap down there.

I'd been so busy that I'd pushed every emotion onto the back burner. That plan had actually been pretty successful until this moment. But now I was standing in front of Avery's house and every single doubt came crawling back to the surface. How could I leave her? How could I move to Colorado and never see her again? Never put my arms around her? Never help her out when she protested but so obviously needed it?

I swallowed and knocked on the front door.

A few moments later, Adeline answered. "Hey, Riv."

"Hey, Addy. Is Avery around?"

"She's just getting off work from the paper, but she called to say that she was on her way. Want to come in and wait?"

Normally I'd say no, that I'd call her, and then I'd intercept her drive home in order to steal a couple quiet moments with her. But since she hadn't answered any of my calls and had replied to my texts with one-word answers, this was probably the only way I'd get any face time with her.

"Yeah, that sounds great," I said, walking into the house. It was nice, spacious enough for a family, and had been built with care, but the last eleven years had been tough on it, and it wasn't like her dad was going to jump up and volunteer to grab a hammer. *Speaking of which, I should fix that bannister while I'm here.*

"Avery? Is that you?" her dad yelled from the living room.

"Nope, Mr. Claire, it's me—River."

"Get in here, boy."

I rolled my eyes at not just his word choice but his tone. I sure as hell was not his boy. My father would have kicked this guy's ass ten times over for the man he'd let himself become. But for Avery, well, I could handle him.

"Sir," I said as I entered the living room. Whoa, there was shit everywhere. Dishes on the coffee table, trash on the floor, and he smelled like he hadn't seen water in at least a week...if not two.

As much as I longed to pick everything up before Avery got home, I knew she'd die of embarrassment. So I did what I learned to do the first year we'd been friends—ignored it.

"You're leaving for Colorado, eh?" he asked, shifting his weight enough to reach for the beer on the floor.

"That appears to be the plan."

"Find greener pastures?" He took a swig, and I briefly wondered if he was mixing the alcohol with his meds, or if Avery had successfully hidden the bottles before she left for work.

"No, sir. My father's old Hotshot crew is restarting, and they can't get the job done without me."

"Well, aren't you just important."

I wanted to sigh, to curse him, to steal Avery away from this life he thought she owed him. Instead, I offered him a tight smile and said, "It's just a numbers game, really."

He grunted. "Well, I imagine Avery will be a little put off."

"I imagine so."

An awkward silence settled over us, which was—thank God— soon interrupted by the sound of the door opening.

"Riv?" Avery's voice carried through the downstairs.

"In here," I answered.

She came through the arch of the living room, all frayed pony-tail and well-worn Beastie Boys T-shirt. "I saw your truck out front. Is everything okay?"

"He just came to see you," her dad answered.

"Oh," she said, looking between the two of us. Then she nodded toward the door.

"It's always a pleasure to see you, Mr. Claire," I said.

"You, too, River. Good luck in Colorado." He hadn't even looked away from the television.

I followed Avery through the hallway and up the stairs, my eyes front and center on the way her shorts hugged the sumptuous curve of her ass. Trying hard to do the right thing, I looked away, but that only took me to the tight, toned thighs that I was already picturing locked around my hips.

She led me into her room and shut the door behind us. I took in the space that still boasted high school and college pictures. "Nothing here changes much," I said.

"It's my own personal time capsule," she replied, sitting on her bed.

I took the chair from her desk, swinging my leg over and sitting on it backwards to keep some kind of barrier between us. Ever since I knew I was leaving, it was like the control I maintained around her—the constant checks I kept on myself and my need for her—was fraying, like my sex drive knew our time was limited. "I like it. It's you."

She laughed in a self-deprecating way that I hated. "Never changing, stuck, and gathering dust."

"Steady and loyal."

We locked eyes, and the zing of electricity between us was palpable. Did she feel it, too? If so, why would she deny it?

Because you've never given her a reason not to, asshole.

"I've been avoiding you," she said, her eyes open and honest.

"I know."

"I don't know how to handle this, and it seemed easier to bury my head in the sand and just not deal." She hugged her pillow to her chest.

"You talk to me. I talk to you. That's how this friendship has always worked."

"But how is it going to work with you in Colorado? I know I'm supposed to be happy for you. This is your dad's crew, and I know what that means to you. But selfishly..." She shook her head.

"What? Don't clam up on me."

She shrugged. "It's just... The day you bought the land to build your house was one of the happiest days of my life."

I blinked. "Wait. What?"

"Stupid, I know."

"I didn't say that. I just don't understand." *Talk to me, Avery.*

"That was what? Three years ago?" she asked.

"About. You were dating that dickhead math major."

Her eyebrows rose. "Good memory."

"I remember everything when it comes to you," I said, then cursed myself when her eyes widened even more. *Smooth. Real smooth.* "The land?" I prompted.

"Right. You buying that land felt like you were putting down roots. That you'd stayed when you graduated—when everyone else left—it felt solid. Dependable."

"Are you talking about me or the house?" Those weren't love words, or even attraction words. Hell, she'd just described my truck.

"You, and it's a good thing. That moment felt like you would always be here, that you were the person I could lean on. I've never looked into my future and not seen you in it. This scares the shit out of me."

I gave up the chair and sat down on the bed next to her. "Me, too. But I can't not go."

She leaned her head on my shoulder, and I rested mine on hers. "I'd never ask you to stay," she whispered. "I know you can't."

"But I can't imagine leaving you, either."

"Then it seems, we are at an impasse."

The clock on my dash changed to 1:36 a.m. I'd been sitting in my truck for the last hour in front of the Golden Eagle Saloon, trying to figure out how to explain the crazy plan I'd concocted between the hours of leaving Avery's house and sitting here now.

The bar closed in twenty-four minutes, so I had exactly that long to pull my shit together before I went in.

The door opened, and I stopped breathing until I saw that it was just two local girls. Kris waved and I unrolled my window.

She climbed up on my running boards and leaned her pretty face into the cab, reeking of alcohol. "Hey, River," she slurred.

"Hey, Kris. What brings you out tonight?"

"It's my birfday."

"Happy birthday. So you're legal now, huh?"

She slow-winked a brown eye at me and then blew her hair out of her eyes. "Yep! What are you doing?"

"Waiting on Avery."

Her head lolled back in exasperation. "You two. Ugh. Why she'd keep a fine piece of man flesh like you in the friend zone is beyond me. I'd climb you like a ladder." She snorted. "Like a ladder. Get it? Because you're a fireman?"

"Absolutely," I answered. The girl was three sheets to the wind, but I'd known her since she could barely drive.

"River, I'm sorry," her friend Lauren called out. "She's trashed."

"I am not!" She licked her lips. "Want me to wait with you? I can keep you plenty busy."

Usually I'd think about it. Kris was a gorgeous girl, and it wasn't like I was celibate. But first, she was drunk, and that was something I never took advantage of, and second, well…she wasn't Avery. I wanted Avery. "Not tonight, but happy birthday. Lauren, can you get her home?"

She nodded and guided her friend off my truck. "Stone-cold sober, no problem. Good to see you, River!"

By the time the girls piled into Lauren's car and left, it was 1:45 a.m. My heart pounded, my stomach dropping slightly just like it did before I walked into a fire, before I took a step that had the potential to change my life.

I was already out of my truck, climbing the steps to the saloon, before I'd decided that I couldn't wait until two. I couldn't wait another second.

I swung the door open and Avery looked up, startled, from where she was washing down a table. "River?"

I didn't answer her, just looked at Mike, who sat at the end of the bar as usual for a Tuesday night. "Mike, go home."

"It isn't two," he said.

"Close enough."

The forty-something guy got off his stool, tossing cash on the bar. "Thanks for the company, Avery."

"No problem," she answered with a smile.

"River," he said as he walked by me.

"Thanks, Mike."

He nodded and left, the door closing behind him. I knew he wasn't drunk—he came here every night to escape his wife, had one beer around eight thirty, and then sipped soda the rest of the night.

Small towns, man. Everyone knew everyone's business.

"What are you doing here?" Avery asked, licking her lips nervously.

"Are you alone?"

"She will be," Maud said as she popped up from behind the bar where she'd obviously been stocking. "You two have fun." She wiggled her eyebrows at Avery. "I'll go out the back and lock it up."

"Maud," Avery pled.

"Nope, not listening!" she sang with her fingers in her ears like she was five. I knew I liked her for a reason. She sang her way through the back door, and then I heard the exterior door close, too.

Avery leaned back against the table, white-knuckling the edges. "So what's so important that it couldn't wait until morning?"

I leaned against the table opposite hers so that there were only a few feet separating us. "I know how to fix our problem."

"Oh, do you? Because short of you not moving to Colorado, and then subsequently hating me because I took away everyone's chance to have that team back, I'm really not seeing where there's an option."

"Option one: I could go seasonal. Live there during the summers and be back here for the winters."

She shook her head before I even finished what I was saying. "Nope. You can't afford that. There are no jobs up here that would take you on that stipulation, even your crew here couldn't. Next brilliant idea?"

"Okay. Then you move to Colorado with me."

Now I was the one gripping the table as her face drained of color. "What? Are you kidding?"

Fuck, was that my heart in my throat, or had I just swallowed something huge? "I've never been more serious."

Silence stretched between us as she blinked at me, her mouth slightly agape, her unreadable eyes never wavering from mine.

"I'm serious, Avery," I repeated quietly.

"I can tell," she answered.

"I've thought it through—"

"Obviously, because I just talked to you twelve hours ago. Seems perfectly thought out."

"You have always wanted to leave here." I started laying out the reasons like I had planned.

"And you know why I can't!" she shouted. "What are you thinking, River? I can't just pick up and leave. I'm not you. I have responsibilities here. I have Adeline and my father to think of."

"I know. I've watched you struggle every day that I've known you, and I've seen you grow into an amazing, strong woman."

"Stop!" She put her hands over her ears and squeezed her eyes shut, little lines appearing between her eyebrows.

I crossed the distance between us, lightly pulling her hands away from her face. "Open your eyes," I begged.

Her eyelids fluttered open to reveal blue eyes swimming with so much emotion that I nearly lost my breath. "Tell me one thing. If it wasn't for Adeline, for your father, and every piece of obligation that anchors you to this place, would you want to come with me?"

Her eyes flickered back and forth, her tell for when she was hashing something out in her head.

Avery had always been immovable in her loyalty to family, her insistence that she was responsible for them both. It was something I'd always loved about her, but now I needed that to give just an inch.

"Would you want to come with me? Get out of here? The Rockies are just as gorgeous, and the sun is a little more dependable. And best of all, you'd have me."

Her eyes flew to mine. "But I'm not free, no matter how pretty you make it sound."

My thumbs lightly stroked the insides of her wrists. "I know our lives aren't prefect, but I'm asking you, in a perfect world—I'm asking you to pretend—if you didn't have the obligations you do, if it was just you and me making this decision, would you want to come with me? Would you take that leap?"

"To Colorado?" she asked.

"To Colorado," I affirmed just in case she thought I meant back to my house for tea.

Her eyes slid shut. "Yes," she whispered.

My breath abandoned me in a rush, my entire body letting go of the tension that had plagued me since Bishop told me we'd have to go. "Oh, thank God."

"But it doesn't matter," she cried, her face distorting as she fought tears. "What I want doesn't matter. That I would give anything to move somewhere new with a fresh start where I'm not 'that drunk's' daughter, or to have the chance to keep you as my best friend...none of it matters. My life is what it is."

"It doesn't have to be." I took her face in my hands, cradling the back of her head.

"It does. What about Adeline? What would she do?"

My chest tightened at the way she always put everyone else first. "She'd come with."

Avery's jaw went slack in my hands. "What?"

"Legacy has a great high school. Brand-new facilities. It's a small town, but there's a kindness there I haven't seen anywhere else. Addy would be welcome there, with us, and so would you. Stop looking at me like I'm dreaming. This is possible."

"You'd bring her with you? With us?"

"Of course. She's a part of you, and she needs to get out just as much as you do."

"And my father?"

My jaw flexed. This had been the one point that had been hard to swallow, but I knew I had to if I wanted to keep Avery in my life. And she was worth any hurdle I had to jump, or any length of broken glass I had to walk across barefoot. I had no doubt the girl standing in front of me was the key to the rest of my life.

"He can come, too," I said softly.

"Now I know you're joking." She tried to pull her face from my hands, but I wouldn't let her. "You hate him."

"I hate how he treats you," I corrected her. "I've never understood why you take it."

"He's Addy's guardian," she explained. "I could never abandon her."

"Then if he's what I have to put up with to keep you in my life, to keep you near, then fine, I'll do it. There are treatment facilities in Colorado, and maybe if we can just get him clean—"

She sobbed—one long whimper, which was the one reaction I wasn't expecting.

"Avery," I whispered. "Don't cry."

"Why? Why would you do that? Drag the worst part of my life into yours?"

A smile tugged up the corners of my lips as I wiped away her single tear that escaped. "Because I get you. I can't leave you. It's never been Bishop keeping me here. It's always been you."

"But why?" she squeaked.

"God, don't you know by now?"

"No," she whispered as something that looked like hope passed through those blue eyes.

"Yes, you do. You've always known, just the same as me." I sent up a quick prayer that she wouldn't smack the hell out of me, and then I kissed her.

She gasped in surprise, and I kept the caress light, taking my time with her lips as I waited for her response. She was so soft. I ran my tongue along her lower lip, savoring the delicate curve. I sipped at her with soft kisses until it hit me—while she was letting me kiss her, she wasn't responding.

My stomach twisted.

I pulled back slowly, scared to see what lingered in her eyes, and prayed it wasn't disgust. What the hell had I been thinking to kiss her like that? We'd never shown any signs of crossing the line, and I'd just jumped across it. Her eyes were closed, giving me no hint of what she was feeling. "Avery?" I asked softly.

Her pulse raced under my hand.

Her eyes fluttered open and there was no anger, just surprise. "You want me?"

"I have *always* wanted you."

With a soft cry, she met my lips, opening hers in a hungry kiss. My tongue swept inside the mouth I'd dreamed of for years, and *holy shit, she tasted* even better than I'd ever fantasized. She tasted faintly of the peppermint tea she loved and pure, sweet Avery.

I explored her mouth with sweeping strokes of my tongue, and she rubbed back against me with every one, creating a friction that sent heat streaking through me, pooling in my dick.

My hands shifted, tilting her head so I could kiss her deeper. If this was the only time I'd get to kiss her, then I was sure-as-fuck going to leave her with a memory that haunted her at night the same way she already did for me. She melted against me, our bodies molding effortlessly into each other.

Holy shit. I'm kissing Avery. And she was kissing me back like her life depended on it. One of my hands left the curve of her face and drifted down her back, giving her every chance to protest—she didn't—before I grasped her ass and lifted her up to set her on the table. I stepped between her outstretched thighs, and she ground against me, moaning into my mouth when she discovered just how much I wanted her.

I'd never been so hard so fast for any woman in my life. But Avery wasn't just any other woman. She was everything I'd ever wanted. The woman I'd compared every girl to. The only one who had my heart without ever knowing it.

She threw her head back, and I pressed kisses down her neck, careful not to mark the tender flesh. We weren't eighteen anymore, and I wasn't going to paw at her like an inexperienced teenager no matter how loudly my body screamed at me that she was finally in my hands.

Her fingers threaded through my hair, and she rocked against my hips and whimpered my name. It was the most beautiful sound I'd ever heard.

I brought my mouth back to hers for one last, long, luscious kiss, pouring everything I had into it. I almost forgot my own name as I gave myself over to everything Avery was.

Then, with the control of a saint, I pulled back from her. She looked up at me with hazy, passion-filled eyes and kiss-stung lips. *Yup, sainthood.*

"River?" she asked, her voice husky and so damn sexy that I had the immediate urge to see what color her panties were and how they'd look on the floor.

Instead I kissed her forehead and took my hands off her—before I fucked my best friend in the bar that she worked at. Avery deserved so much better than that, and for how long I'd waited, I did, too.

"I want you," I said, my voice so low I barely recognized it.

Her mouth opened to speak, and I pressed my thumb against her tempting lips.

"Don't say anything. I just wanted you to know that you have options. That *I* am an option. And whether it's in friendship or something more, I want you in Colorado with me. I leave next week for a weekend there, and I've already bought you a ticket. It's just a weekend—not a lifetime commitment, but I want you to come and see if you could make a life there. A life with me or without me—that's your choice."

I stroked her lip with my thumb and leaned forward, stealing one more kiss. "God, I've waited so many years to do that."

"River…"

"Don't," I ordered softly. "Don't talk. Just think. I'll wait outside for you to lock up, and then maybe we can talk tomorrow?"

She nodded, and I backed away slowly, refusing to notice the rapid rise and fall of her breasts, or that her lips were still parted like she was waiting for me to come back and kiss the hell out of her again.

Maybe I'd just fucked everything up. Maybe I'd thrown away the best relationship of my life by pushing for something that she didn't want, but when I looked back and saw her touching her lips as I walked out the door, I couldn't help but smile.

Maybe I'd just made the best decision of my life.

4
AVERY

I flipped through the magazine at Dr. Stone's office, not really seeing the print on the pages. My mind was too focused on River.

He'd kissed me. My eyes slid shut as I remembered his lips against mine, the feel of his tongue, his hands, his sweet taste. My fingertips slid over my lips like I could still feel him there.

How could one moment change everything?

Just like that.

It had been the best kiss of my life—hot enough that had he not stopped us, I wasn't sure where we would have ended up.

On the table. The bar. His bed.

I felt heat rush to my face and opened my eyes, smiling. He made me happy, which was something I hadn't been in such a long time. Kissing him hadn't been the awkward first kiss of friends trying out something more. It had been like two magnets finally flipped so they were unable to do anything but collide.

"What has you all smiley?" Dad grumbled, sitting on the exam table.

"River," I answered honestly. He'd texted me all day yesterday from work, but our schedules hadn't meshed and we hadn't gotten a chance to see each other.

His eyes narrowed. "Don't get too attached to that boy, Avery. He'll just break your heart when he leaves, and you'll be downright bitchy. Hell, it's bad enough already." He pointed at me. "Watch yourself."

I soothed my hackles, which begged to go up in my own defense. "Actually, I think I'm going to Colorado with him next weekend."

Dad's mouth hung open, his eyes ready to shoot fire. "You. Are. Not."

"I am," I said with a certainty I hadn't felt this morning when I woke up. *Guess you made that decision.* "It's just for a weekend, Dad. Aunt Dawn already said she'd come up and stay." She'd actually been all too happy to do so when I'd called her this morning.

"You can not put her out like that!"

"Dad, she lives thirty minutes away and she's retired. It's hardly putting her out to ask her to spend a weekend with her brother."

He grumbled, tapping his foot against the side of the exam table. "And what about Adeline?"

"What about her?" I closed the magazine, giving up any pretense of reading.

"Are you thinking of moving there? With him? Why else would you go?"

I should have waited until we were home to say anything, or told him before this appointment. "Let's just talk about this later."

"No, the doc is late as usual. Let's talk about it now." He crossed his arms around his chest. His fingernails were too long, but at least I'd gotten him to shower this morning.

For the smallest second, the potential of a different future washed over me—a future where every day wasn't fighting with him, where I could live for me, step fully into the independent adulthood I'd always been so scared to want. A future where River kissed me, where I finally allowed myself to really examine my feelings for my best friend.

"What if I wanted to move?" I asked softly. "What if I wanted to have an actual life, Dad?"

"One where you're not tied down by an invalid father? Is that what you mean?"

"You're not an invalid. And River already said you could come with us—"

"Enough!" he snapped. "I'm not moving to Colorado and neither are you. Your life is here, with me. I know it's not the life you wanted, but this isn't what I wanted, either. We're in this together. It's always been you and me, Avery. What would I do without you? What would Adeline do? You know we can't make it without you. So you can go for the weekend and live out your little fantasy, but you know you'll come right back here, because you're not the kind of girl to walk out on her family."

He lifted his eyebrows, challenging me to say that I was.

Was he right? Did it matter what I wanted?

The doctor knocked, saving me from going down that tunnel.

"Mr. Claire," Dr. Stone said as he sat in front of the computer on the desk and flipped through the screens. "Okay, so how have you been feeling this month? Your weight is up."

"I like to eat," Dad joked, bringing out his charming side, the way he always did with Dr. Stone. After all, he had something Dad wanted.

He's playing you, too.

I kept my thoughts to myself as Dr. Stone examined him, prodding and asking the same questions he did every month.

"And how is your pain level?" he asked.

They had my full attention, now.

"It's bad, doc," Dad said, grimacing as he pushed against his lower back. "It's getting worse."

Dr. Stone nodded thoughtfully, rubbing his goatee. It was hard to believe he was the same age as my dad, or maybe it was just that there were healthy men that age, in general. "I'm not going to lie to you, Jim. The pain is always going to be there. There's no guarantee with a spine fused where yours is. I know it hurts."

"Can we up my meds? Give me a little relief?"

Dr. Stone sighed and sat back at the computer, going through the screens again. "I really think you're at your max on the opioids. I can't safely prescribe any more without putting you at risk for overdose."

"It hurts," Dad snapped, startling me. He never showed his angry face outside the house. No, that side of him was reserved for Adeline and me, of course.

"I know," Dr. Stone said, leaning back in his chair. "Maybe it's time to discuss other options."

"Something stronger?" Dad suggested.

For the love. If they got Dad any higher, he'd be an astronaut.

"No, but there are new methods out there. Ways of going directly after the nerves." He tilted his head. "And we should look at your weight. Other patients with this same fusion live relatively active, normal lives. Yes, they're still in pain—that is absolutely real, but we've been able to decrease pain meds by natural means."

"Well, I'm not interested in that. I want it to stop hurting. Now. So can you help me?"

Dr. Stone looked at me, and I dropped my eyes. The repercussions from outing Dad would be disastrous at home. "Avery, can I talk with you outside?"

"Why do you want to talk to her alone?" Dad questioned.

"Just some caregiver stuff. She still has your medical power of attorney, right?"

"Yes," Dad grumbled.

"Then there shouldn't be an issue, right? Unless there's something you don't want me to know?"

"It's fine," Dad answered.

Shit.

I didn't need to look at Dad to know that his eyes bore into me. Hell, I could feel the heat from here.

Dr. Stone shut the door behind us as we stepped into the hallway. "How is he, really?" he asked.

Angry. Drunk. Verbally abusive. Legally Adeline's guardian.

"Fine."

"Avery?" He gave me the Dad tone he'd probably used on his daughter Michelle...Michelle who'd gone to college in Texas after we'd both graduated. Michelle who, no doubt, had a life.

I could lie, send Dad further down the rabbit hole. Or I could take the smallest step to force some change into his life. If not for my own good, then Addy's.

"He's angry," I said, my eyes dropping to the floor as I betrayed the only parent I had left. "He drinks too much, he won't get off the couch, and the farthest he'll go is for the remote unless we're coming here on our monthly trip to refill his meds."

"Jesus," he muttered.

"You asked," I said, raising my eyes. "He's destroying himself."

"And taking you down with him," he noted.

I shook my head. "It's not about me. But it is about Adeline."

He nodded slowly.

"I need you to keep this between us," I whispered.

He sighed, rubbing the bridge of his nose. "Okay. Thank you for being honest with me."

I took a deep breath and hardened my defenses as we walked back in. Between this and the bombshell of going to Colorado that I'd just dropped on him, I might need some of those pain meds for the headache all his yelling would give me.

"Well, Avery says nothing much has changed," Dr. Stone forced a smile. "We'll keep you on the same dose you're at. I don't want you in pain, but let's explore some of those other treatments, shall we? I want you to go back to physical therapy. Really make a go of it this time."

"No," Dad said simply, like the doc had asked him if he wanted mashed potatoes with dinner.

Dr. Stone scribbled on his pad and then ripped off the sheet as he gave Dad a smile. "Well, I'm not asking. If you want me to refill this prescription next month, you'll call this number," he said, adding a business card to the sheet as he handed it to Dad. "Dr. Maxwell is great, and I'll check in with her to make sure you're attending whatever sessions she recommends before we meet again next month."

Dad's eyes snapped toward mine. "What did you say?"

"Dad," I pled. It was shitty enough having the hermit, drunk dad who everyone talked about, but public embarrassment? That was a new level of hell I hadn't had since I'd had to pull him off a barstool at the Golden Saloon when I was sixteen.

Now I worked there.

"She said you're doing well on these meds, but your pain has you uncomfortable, Jim," Dr. Stone answered. "This isn't a punishment. We're looking for a long-term solution for you to return to feeling fully functional. Physical therapy is going to help strengthen your back muscles and maybe lose a little of that weight. It will be good for you. Good for the girls who are taking such good care of you, too."

Dad grunted.

Because the truth was he hadn't cared about us in such a long time that I wasn't sure he knew how to anymore.

"Oh em gee!" Adeline squealed and danced around me, acting every single day of her thirteen years.

"Shhh!" I said as we made our way out to my car.

"You can't shush me!" she said, taking the passenger seat as I climbed into the driver's side.

"I can, too."

"No way! You and River! Finally!"

I could practically see the hearts dancing above her head. "Stop!" I laughed. "Look, I only told you because I need to make sure that you're okay with Aunt Dawn coming up next weekend to stay with you."

"Absolutely. Dad will be on his best behavior with her in the house."

She chatted on, stating easily a dozen times that she couldn't believe it took us this long to get together. I reminded her every single time that it was just a kiss and we weren't together.

"Yes, you are. You're going away together!"

"I'm going with him to check out his home town and see where he'll be living. He doesn't know how soon he'll have to move." *Too soon.*

"You should go with him," she said, playing with her phone.

"What?" I said, my hands tightening on the wheel.

"You. Should. Go. Get the hell out of here."

"Don't swear," I said automatically. "And that's a huge thing to even think about."

"Why? Because life is *so* great here?" She snorted. "Seriously. If you have a chance to get out, do it. I'm leaving the first chance I get."

"You're not happy?"

She shrugged, her eyes still on that damn phone. "Sure. But it's not like I have a ton of friends. Everything is"—she shrugged again—"stagnant. Nothing changes. It feels like one of those ponds that just grows crap and mosquitos."

"But there are good things, too, right?"

"Yeah, of course. You're here, and it's nice to see Aunt Dawn when she comes around. But I'm not going to stay here. I'm leaving for college, and then once I've seen what's out there, maybe I'll come back. But I don't want to feel like I stayed because it was the only option. You're not mad, are you?" She looked over at me.

"Not at all," I said as we turned onto her friend's street. "I had those exact thoughts at your age."

"But then Mom died."

I nodded slowly. "Then Mom died." *And my entire future went with her.*

I pulled into the driveway and put the car in park, quickly touching Adeline's wrist before she could open her door. "Addy, if it was your choice, would you go? If you were me?"

"In a heartbeat," she said without blinking. "Dad puts you through hell. Once River leaves…I just think you deserve a chance to be happy. Both of you do."

My heart stuttered, knowing I needed to ask her. I couldn't make these kinds of choices without her. "Okay, and if there was a way for you to come with me? Would you? I know it's more complicated than that, and that you have friends and a life, and Dad, but just for the purpose of this conversation, would you?"

She tilted her head in a way that reminded me so much of our mother. "I'd pack a box tomorrow. In theory."

"In theory," I repeated.

She lunged across the console of my SUV and kissed me on the cheek. "Don't hurt your brain, sis. Catch you later?"

"Yeah."

A couple I-love-yous later, I left her at Mandy's for the sleepover. My thoughts raced as I drove. What would it even take to bring her with me? *If you go.* I couldn't leave Adeline. I could barely process the thought of leaving Dad. It didn't matter how far he'd sunk, he was still my dad.

I would have given anything for five minutes with Mom. What would happen if I left here, lost him, and had that same regret?

I'd parked in front of River's house before I even realized I was headed there. I meant to go home, but I guessed my subconscious knew what I really needed.

Zeus didn't bark as I approached the door, so I knew he wasn't inside. That meant he was out for a run with River. My hand paused on the door handle. Was I allowed to just walk in anymore? I still had a key, of course, but we'd done some really weird transitioning, and I didn't know where we stood.

Keys for best friends? No big deal.

A key for your girlfriend? Huge. Like iceberg and *Titanic* huge.

Like moving to Colorado huge.

I opted for the three o'clock sun, which hung directly above me, and stretched my legs out on the steps that led to the porch. Peace seeped into me in the quiet, filling more of my chest with each breath, spreading through me in the way only being near River—or even just his house—could.

Gravel crunched nearby, and my breath caught as I opened my eyes. *Holy. Shit.* River ran with Zeus unleashed at his side, his strides eating up the ground as he came closer.

He was shirtless, all of that gorgeous, bronzed skin basking in the sunlight. I'd always known he was hot. I wasn't blind to the girls who flocked to him, or my own attraction. But my need to check my own drool level was new. The tribal tattoo that stretched across his chest rippled with his movements, and as he came toward me, I made out the tiny rivulets of sweat that slipped down the cut lines of his torso to his carved abs.

The man was a walking advertisement for sex.

I shifted my legs under me as he slowed, a smile spreading across his face. "Hey, you," he said, breathing heavily but not over-exerted.

"Hi," I said, suddenly shy. The last time we'd spoken had been right after he'd pulled his tongue out of my mouth.

The way he looked at me—blatant hunger in those brown eyes —made me feel like he was thinking the same exact thing.

"What are you doing out here?" he asked as Zeus licked my face.

"Waiting for you."

His forehead puckered, but he pulled me to my feet easily. "Good answer, want to come in?"

I nodded, and he led us inside, heading straight for the kitchen. He pulled two bottles of water out of the fridge and offered one to me. "No thank you," I said, scared that if I drank the water it would come right back up in a second.

"Okay," he said, then chugged the water.

Damn, even the muscles of his throat were sexy.

"So why were you sitting on my porch like some kind of stranger? You have a key," he said as he put the empty bottle into the recycling bin.

"I feel like that key just became complicated," I said, dragging my eyes up the muscles of his back as he turned away to grab the other bottle. I knew Bishop pushed him at the gym, but damn. Just...*damn*. In the past, he'd always thrown a shirt on around me unless we were at the lake, and to be honest, I hadn't looked.

No point wanting what you knew you couldn't have.

But now I could have him. It was like seven years of pent-up sexual frustration were hitting me all at once, smashing the walls of my defenses with a battering ram made out of pure steel...kind of like his body.

"Uncomplicate it. You have a key, so use it."

He hit me with those eyes, and I nearly melted. Was this the charm the other girls at the bar raved about? Had he simply never used it on me before?

"You gave it to me...you know...before."

"Before what?" he asked.

I blew my breath out through a rumble of my lips. "Come on, you know."

His smirk sent my panties up in flames. *Good thing he knows how to put those out.* "Say it."

"Before you kissed me and I stopped being best-friend Avery and turned into...I don't even know. Kissable Avery?"

He stalked forward until he stood just a breath away, close enough to touch, but not. "You have always been kissable Avery, I've just never been allowed to kiss you like I wanted. You're also fuckable Avery—"

"River!" My cheeks ran hot.

His grin was wide and so very beautiful. "Oh no, I have nothing to lose. I'm done pulling my punches. Done being careful around you. Done trying my best not to let it show how badly I want you."

Oh God, he was *good*. His words alone had me ready to strip him in the kitchen. *Or maybe that's a year plus without sex.*

"Okay," I whispered. *Lame.*

He stroked my cheek with his thumb. "But you're still best-friend Avery. That's never going to change no matter how many times I get to kiss you or how often you'll let me touch you. If you decide that was the only kiss we'll ever share, you'll still be my best friend."

The thought soured my stomach. "You'd be okay if I cut you off?"

"No. I'd just work my ass off to convince you otherwise."

"Oh."

"Oh," he repeated, and kissed my forehead lightly before backing away.

A stab of disappointment hit me right between my thighs.

"So what made you stop by?" He looked at his phone and put it right down. "I know you have to be to work in twenty minutes."

"I just kind of ended up here."

"That's okay. I like seeing you." He lifted the second bottle of water to his lips and took a sip, never once looking away.

There was something so ordinary about the motion, the ease there was between us that made me long for a different future— made me wonder if it was possible to change my course in life.

"I'll go," I said suddenly. "For the weekend," I corrected.

"Really?" His face lit up like the time I'd given him Mumford & Sons concert tickets for his birthday.

"Yes," I answered.

I was in his arms before I finished the word as he swung me around the kitchen against his very hot, very sweaty chest. "You're going to love it!" he promised as we spun.

Laughter bubbled from my chest, and I felt lighter than I had in years, like he'd picked up more than my weight—he'd lifted my soul.

"Can I kiss you?" he asked, his eyes dropping to my lips.

"Yes," I said. "But you'd better make it fast. I have to leave in five minutes."

I sighed when his lips brushed over mine, relearning the feel of them. Then our mouths opened, and the sweet kiss turned hot so fast my head spun.

Good God, the man could kiss.

He consumed my every thought, until my only concerns were how close I could get and how much deeper I could kiss him.

Finally he pulled my hands from around his neck. "You'd better go before I keep you here with me."

"I'm not sure I would mind."

He groaned and set me down, backing away slowly. "Go. Now. Just be ready for the perfect trip to Colorado, because then you're mine."

"I like the way that sounds...*mine.*"

"Me, too," he said softly.

This was good. No, this was better than anything I'd ever felt. And when he looked at me like that—like he'd been waiting a lifetime to sample me and now he was planning his attack—I melted.

How had we done this? Flipped from friends to horny teens in the span of two days?

"Go, Avery." He ran his tongue along his lower lip, and I knew if I stayed a moment longer I'd never make it to work. Ever.

I ran.

5
RIVER

*D*amn, that thing was long. I looked back at the trench we'd dug in to the south side of the fire and examined it for weak spots. We'd chosen the only feasible place to dig in and tried to clear as much of the fuel as possible.

"You good?" Bishop asked, sliding his chainsaw into its case.

"Yeah, finished." Sweat ran in rivulets along my face. I couldn't wait to get down from this ridgeline and get my helmet off.

The fire was a small one compared to our last blaze, but when the call had gone out shortly after Avery left my house, I'd answered. I would always answer. I thought of it as my last hoorah with the Midnight Sun crew.

I'd also cursed like a fucking sailor. This fire, as small as it was, had cost me four days with Avery. Maybe in the larger scheme of things, four days didn't mean much. But when I was only guaranteed a couple of weeks with her, four days was forever.

"Let's get out of here," Bishop said, hoisting his chainsaw to his shoulder.

I gave the ridgeline one last look. Would this be the last time I was called to the Alaskan wilderness? It was a bittersweet thought. Next year this time I'd be on the Legacy crew, as long as we could pull back the numbers the council wanted.

"River?" Bishop called as the team started down the mountain.

"Yeah, I'm coming," I said, turning to join the line of guys. If we got down in the next couple hours, there was a chance we'd make it back in time for me to see Avery tonight.

"You ready to head home?" Bishop asked as I fell in next to him.

"Which one?" I asked.

"Both, I guess."

"I'm ready to see Avery."

A grin spread across his face. "So that's how it is now, eh?"

"To be honest, I don't really know how it is. She agreed to come to Colorado for the weekend, so I'll take it."

"And anything else she has to offer?" He shot me a little side-eye.

"I'll take anything she's willing to give," I answered softly.

Never one to talk about his feelings, Bishop's jaw tightened. His mouth opened and closed a few times, until it was downright painful to watch.

"For fuck's sake, just say it. Whatever it is."

"Do you want to reconsider the Legacy crew? You have a life here, a house, a great team, and a great girl. I wouldn't think any less of you if you didn't want to go."

I thought about it—the simple act of staying. I loved Midnight Sun, my house, the landscape...hell, even the crazy hours the sun kept were growing on me. Staying gave me a shot at keeping Avery, really seeing what we could turn into. If being in a relationship was as easy as being her best friend, then I knew we could be extraordinary. But as certain as I was of how perfect we'd be, I also knew that the actual chances of her moving with me were insanely small.

She'd never leave her father, and he'd never agree to move.

But if I didn't go, Legacy wouldn't get her Hotshot crew back, and I'd lose the last piece of my father. So would Bishop and every other Legacy kid.

So I was pretty much fucked either way.

"River?" Bishop asked again as we continued our descent.

"Sorry, just a lot on my mind. I haven't changed my mind about the crew. I'm just hoping that visiting Colorado is enough to make Avery want to come with."

Bishop whistled low. "That's a lot to ask of a girl you've been dating for a week."

Were we dating? We hadn't really had the whole "what are we" talk. "It's a Hail Mary. The whole thing with her is, but I couldn't just leave and not try."

"You're in love with her."

My grip tightened on the axe handle. "How long have you known?"

He shrugged, moving the chainsaw. "Since the first day we were here. I figured you'd get your shit straight sooner or later."

"It's pretty much the latest moment possible."

"Yeah, well, we don't remember the easily won games, right? The victories we remember are the ones where the outcome came down to the last minute, the overtime."

"The Hail Mary," I said.

He slapped my back. "The Hail Mary."

The bar was busy for a Tuesday, but it was Ladies Night, which brought the women out for the drinks, and the men out for the ladies.

I made my way through the crowd and took a tall table at the back, sitting so I could see Avery at the bar.

Fuck, she was beautiful. Her hair was up in a ponytail, swishing with her every movement as she poured drinks.

"So you and Avery, huh?" Jessie said, grabbing the empty chair to my right.

"How did you know?" I asked, my eyes still locked on Avery. She went up on her tiptoes to grab a bottle off the shelf, giving me a perfect view of her ass, and I sucked in a breath reflexively. We were in a room with at least thirty of our neighbors. Common sense told me that this wasn't the place for me to ogle, let alone fantasize about propping her up on the bar and sliding her jeans down her thighs so I could taste her. I'd never had an issue controlling myself around Avery. Sure, my body had always reacted to the sight of her, but now that I'd had a taste and knew that she wanted the same thing…well, my body was trying to overrule my common sense.

And the bar really was perfect height.

"Please. Like you can keep a secret in this town? Just about everyone has seen the way you guys have been looking at each other these last few years. We were just waiting for Avery to find the courage to say something and you to stop fucking around in Fairbanks with co-eds.

"The way we look at each other?" I parroted, focusing in on Avery. I could see how I'd been obvious. Hell, I couldn't take my eyes off her if we were in the same room—hence my cycle of breakups—but Avery had never once hinted that she wanted more than what we had. If she'd so much as breathed in my direction, I would have jumped before she said how high.

But she'd never thrown me signals. Maybe that was one of the reasons this whole situation was terrifying. Was she only kissing me back because she didn't want to lose her best friend? Was I pushing her for something she didn't really want?

Feeling unsure of myself was a foreign concept and damned inconvenient seeing as I had less than a week in Colorado to convince her to uproot her whole life for me.

"Please." Jessie snorted, playing with her beer bottle. "You look at her like you're ready to eat her alive."

"Fair assessment," I admitted, done hiding how I felt about her. I swallowed, my throat suddenly tight. "And her?"

"Seriously?" She arched an eyebrow at me.

"Seriously."

"She looks at you like you're everything she's ever wanted, dipped in chocolate and ready for a tasty bite. Always has."

I ripped my eyes from Avery to look at Jessie. She nodded slowly as she laughed. "You should see your face right now. If your jaw was any lower you'd be hitting the floor."

My gaze whipped back and forth between the two women. Avery looked at me? Why the hell hadn't I noticed? Was I blind? Or was she really that good at hiding her feelings?

"Never thought I'd see the day where River Maldonado was speechless."

"First time for everything," I said softly. Maybe this would work. Maybe she really did want me enough to leave. My mind raced with different scenarios as I swiped open my phone. She could stay through the school year if Addy needed that much time, or just to give her dad a few more months to come around, and be in Colorado by summer. I'd have the house set up by then, and they could stay with me until they figured out what they wanted to do.

Or maybe Avery would never move out. Maybe my house would become *our* house.

My chest tightened to the point of pain as she smiled at Maud. I couldn't push her too fast—just because I'd been in love with her for the last seven years didn't mean that she felt the same. But I didn't exactly have another option with the deadline for the Legacy crew.

As much as I loved watching her, I also couldn't wait another minute to get my arms around her.

River: WHAT ARE YOU UP TO?

I hit send and watched as she pulled out her cell phone, grinning as her thumbs worked on the small device.

Avery: WORKING. YOU? HOW IS THE FIRE?

River: FIRE'S ONE HUNDRED PERCENT CONTAINED. I'M THINKING ABOUT TAKING THIS REALLY HOT BLONDE OUT.

Her eyebrows puckered together and her face fell.

River: IT'S DEFINITELY THE GREEN RIBBON IN HER HAIR THAT HAS ME TURNED ON.

Her eyes shot up, wide and excited as she scanned the bar, her ribbon moving with the swish of her ponytail.

She jumped when she saw me, racing around the end of the bar. I had barely pushed away from the table and stood when she was in my arms, all sweet-smelling and soft.

"Hey, baby," I said into her hair as I held her to me, lifting her against my chest.

She wrapped those incredible legs around my waist and burrowed her face into my neck. "River." She sighed my name like a prayer. "Why didn't you tell me you were back?"

"I wanted to surprise you," I said, easily supporting her weight and loving the feel of her pressed against me.

Her arms tightened around me, and her fingers moved through my hair, lightly scratching my scalp. "I was so worried."

Damn, I loved her. "I was fine. Promise. I'm sorry we were out of service up there, but it really was an easy one."

"Good. I didn't know if you'd make it home before we had to leave."

I urged her back and she met my eyes. "Nothing's going to stop me from taking you to Colorado this weekend."

Nothing. Not her dad, or even Addy—as much as I adored her. This weekend was for us.

Her eyes dropped to my lips and want slammed into me, more intense than any time I'd ever come home from a fire. "Keep looking at me like that and you'll get kissed in front of all these people. I've never minded gossip, but you might."

Her tongue snuck out to wet her lower lip. "I don't care."

Fuck it. My fingers threading through the base of her ponytail, I crushed her mouth to mine. I tried to remember where we were, that I couldn't strip her down in the middle of a crowded bar. I tried to keep the kiss short, just enough to satisfy the craving I'd had for her mouth since I'd been called away.

I failed.

Her tongue moved against mine and I was gone. I sank into her, tilting her head so I could find a deeper, sweeter angle, and I forgot where we were. Hell, I forgot there was anyone else on the planet besides us.

Her ass pushed into my hand as she arched, her breasts stealing my breath as they pressed against me. She made that sexy little noise in the back of her throat, and I was ready to carry her the hell out of there and take her in my damned truck if it meant the throbbing in my dick would ease up just a little.

Someone cleared her throat, and I remembered that we were, in fact, the very opposite of being alone. I pulled away, but Avery held my lip with gentle suction, her teeth grazing the skin lightly as she finally released me.

Holy. Fucking. Shit.

My breathing was too fast, too uncontrolled, and I was way too turned on to be this public at the moment.

"Welcome home," she whispered, those blue eyes hazy with passion and happiness.

"I love the sound of that," I admitted as I let her down. Her curves rubbed against me every. Inch. Of. The. Way. "You're killing me."

"Feeling's mutual."

"It's about damn time!" someone in the bar called out.

He was followed by a round of applause that had Avery burying her beautiful, flushed face in my shirt. "Yeah, yeah," I said as the clapping died down.

"Oh my God," she mumbled.

I tilted her chin and kissed her scrunched nose. "I'd better get out of here and get packed for tomorrow."

"You are cutting it pretty close."

"Yeah, well, you know me. I have to do everything at the last possible second." *Like tell you that I want you.*

She grinned and kissed me lightly. "Pick me up in the morning?"

"Wouldn't miss it."

I kissed her goodbye just because I could, then made my way to the door before I ended up kissing her again. She waved when I looked back, and suddenly the eight-or-so hours I had to wait to kiss her again seemed like an eternity.

She was all I thought about as I packed a small suitcase and tried to get a few hours of sleep. After the last seven years, it was hard to believe that everything would come down to the next few days.

I had to find a way to convince her that she'd be happy in Colorado—that I was worth the risk. It wasn't a small thing I was asking. Hell no. I wanted her to uproot her whole life and transplant it thousands of miles away, all because I knew that the only way we'd thrive was together.

But what if her dad wouldn't come?

What if she wouldn't leave him?

The clock ticked steadily on the nightstand, reminding me that I had to be up in a matter of hours, but that didn't stop my brain, or the nauseating turn of my stomach that reminded me that no matter how much I loved her, she'd never abandon her family.

I couldn't let my dad's crew die before it even had the chance to be resurrected, but I also knew I'd be a shell of who I was if Avery stayed in Alaska.

I had to make these next few days as perfect as possible.

6

AVERY

"What do you mean you've lost our bags?" River asked the airline attendant as we leaned against the counter the next day. After a delayed flight from Fairbanks, to running through the Seattle airport and barely making our connection to Denver, and then taking the smallest plane I'd ever been willing to get on to Gunnison...well, this trip was definitely off to a rocky start.

We'd been traveling for ten hours, and as happy as I was to be here and to see River's hometown, I was also about to go full-on zombie apocalypse raid on that vending machine in the lobby if we didn't find some food soon.

"I've tracked them as currently in route from Seattle to Denver, sir," the small girl said as she pushed her glasses up her nose with a look that pretty much said, *please don't eat me.*

Not that River was intimidating. *Liar.* River was huge and rather cranky at the moment. "It's okay." I put my hand on his bicep.

"It's not okay," he told me. "All your stuff—"

"I can buy what I need until it gets here." I looked over to the girl who was furiously typing. "Can you have it delivered to Legacy when it gets here?"

She nodded. "Absolutely. The next flight comes in from Denver…" She typed, her eyes never going higher than River's chest. "Tomorrow morning at seven thirty."

"You have got to be kidding—"

I squeezed his arm lightly, then looped mine through it and hugged myself to his side. "That will be just fine."

Her fingers flew over the keyboard as she took down our contact information. With each moment, River grew more tense, until I thought his muscles might snap under my fingers.

The attendant's eyes widened to impossible dimensions when she looked behind us, and I turned my head. Bishop walked toward us, a scowl deepening with every step he took. Maybe I wasn't the only one getting hangry over here.

"What's wrong?" River asked.

"All the rental cars are gone. They overbooked or something."

"How is that even possible?" River snapped.

"It's pretty much just par for the course today," I responded, laughter bubbling up.

They both looked at me like I was nuts.

"I called Knox, and he's on his way here. We've probably got about another forty-five minutes before he shows up."

"Perfect, just in time to grab food!" I said.

"Actually, the airport café closed about a half hour ago. I'm so sorry," the attendant said, cringing as all of our gazes swung to her. "They close after the last flight of the day...which was yours."

River's jaw locked. "It's only eight."

"Small airport."

"Let's go wait outside," I said. "I've never seen the sunset in Colorado." *Or anywhere outside of Alaska.* I plastered a smile on my face and prayed it was enough to convince River to leave the poor girl alone. It wasn't her fault that we'd had rotten luck today.

A slight tug on River's arm and he followed me out, Bishop on his heels.

A Snickers bar later I felt somewhat human. River slipped my forefinger into his mouth, licking away the last of the chocolate on my skin, and my thighs clenched. He ran his teeth over the digit and released it, smirking at the way my mouth hung open.

"I'm so sorry today has been a disaster," he said, running his fingers through the strands of my travel-abused ponytail. The evening breeze wrapped a few strands around my neck, and he chased them as we sat on a bench outside.

"This isn't a disaster," I told him. "It's just a kaleidoscope of inconveniences."

"Kaleidoscopes are beautiful."

"And so is this. Think of it this way. We just finished a delicious bit of chocolate as we're watching the sun set behind the Rocky Mountains. The weather is gorgeous, and this just might be the best first date I've ever had."

A corner of his mouth tilted upward. "First date, huh?"

"What would you call it?"

"A sneak peek."

"At what?"

"Everything we could have," he whispered and then brushed his lips over mine, his tongue tracing my bottom lip. Was I ever going to get tired of kissing him? I only craved more and more. For that matter, what was the appropriate amount of time I had to wait before I could kiss other places on his body? Where was the rule book that governed *hey, I know we just got into a relationship, but I've wanted to lick your abs for years?*

I sucked in a breath as he pulled away, my chest burning. "Wow, even just kissing you makes me breathless."

He laughed. "That, my dear Avery, is the altitude. But I'll absolutely take credit. We're almost at eight thousand feet here, and almost nine where we're headed."

"Easier to get you drunk at," Bishop said as he came around the corner.

My cheeks flamed, wondering how much he'd seen.

"No worries," he said as if he'd read my mind. "I've been waiting on you two to get your shit together for years. And there's Knox," he said as a black SUV pulled up to the curb.

"How can you tell?" River asked.

"We're the only ones here, and they locked the airport doors twenty minutes ago."

"Good point," River answered as we stood. When an incredibly hot guy got out and headed toward us, River pulled me under his arm.

Subtle.

"Knox," Bishop said as the two shook hands and then hugged in that tight guy way with lots of back-slapping.

"Good to see you, Bishop." Knox turned his eyes on River and grinned before pulling him into a hug. "River. Damn, you're huge. What the hell are they feeding you up in Alaska?" he asked.

"Moose, mostly," he joked.

Knox held his hand out to me, and I shook it as he made an obvious appraisal. "And who might you be?"

"Avery," I said with a smile. The guy was gorgeous in a Scott Eastwood kind of way, with eyes that held laughter and the promise of a really good time.

"She's with me," River said, pulling me to his side.

"Obviously." Knox grinned and nodded toward the car. "We're about forty-five minutes from home. Let's get you guys settled in and then figure everything out."

We loaded into the back of the SUV, and as we pulled onto the highway out of town, the gentle hum of the car on the pavement sent my exhaustion into sleepville. When my head bobbed for the third time, River unbuckled my seat belt and slid me over to his side, buckling me in the middle.

"Get some rest," he ordered softly.

My head hit the perfect place just under his shoulder. With his warmth and steady heartbeat, I was asleep before a second song could play on the radio.

I vaguely felt River's strong arms lifting me and the crisp mountain air brushing over my skin as he carried me somewhere. "It's okay, you can sleep. I've got you," he said, kissing my forehead.

A few blinks later we were in a hotel room. I brought the room into focus as he lowered me onto the bed. "Food or sleep?" he asked, setting my backpack down on the floor.

I weighed my options, but the three hours of sleep I'd had coupled with the long travel and altitude won out. "Sleep. What about you?"

"It's already ten. I'm game for sleep if you are." He leaned over me, brushing a kiss against my hairline. "I'll be next door with Bishop, just let me know if you need anything, okay?"

A sharp flash of panic hit me when he pulled away. We were in Colorado, where he would be moving, and while I had him now, nothing was guaranteed past this weekend. "Stay with me?" I asked.

"Avery," he whispered, his dark brown eyes soft in the lamplight. He stroked my cheek with his thumb.

"It wouldn't be the first time we've slept together."

A smirk played across his face. "Yeah, well…"

"That's not what I meant." But now that the words were out there…well, would it be a bad idea?

River was undeniably sexy. Hell, my heart rate picked up just thinking about what his hands would feel like on my skin. His lips were sinful, and the look in his eyes told me he wanted me just as much as I wanted him. I knew, without so much as removing a single item of clothing, that we would be incredible together.

Explosive.

"River?" I whispered.

His eyes narrowed slightly as he decided. "You know how badly I want you?"

"I think so."

"I can control myself, Avery. I'm not going to pounce on you, but there's every chance that we could cross a line you're not ready for."

I ran my hands through his hair, the black strands stopping just above his chin. "I know. But if I only have this little bit of time with you, I don't want to give any of it up. Even if we're both sleeping."

He nodded slowly. "Agreed."

I cracked the unsexiest yawn in the history of yawns, and he chuckled.

There was a knock at the door and he answered it, taking a plastic bag from Bishop. "That's all they had downstairs, sorry, man. The bags should be here in the morning."

"I just wanted it to be…"

"Perfect?" Bishop asked, his voice low.

"Yeah, and it's anything but. Could one more thing get fucked up?"

"Let's not chance fate," Bishop said before saying a quiet good night and shutting the door.

River disappeared into the bathroom momentarily. "Avery, there's toothpaste and stuff in the bathroom if you want it, okay?" He said as he came back out.

Shirtless.

Holy shit. I'd always appreciated his body. How could I not? But seeing those yards of muscle and soft, inked skin, and knowing that I could touch them were two different things.

"Teeth. Right." I nodded, forcing myself from the bed. My feet felt like they weighed a bajillion pounds, but I brushed my teeth with the new toothbrush and got ready for bed.

Wait. What the hell was I going to sleep in? Capris and a blouse weren't really conducive to the whole REM thing. River's T-shirt lay folded on the counter, and my fingers caressed the soft cotton. *Perfect.*

A few minutes later I walked out of the bathroom to see River sitting up in bed reading the book he'd brought along. He did a double take as I came into his line of sight, and warmth rushed through me.

He really wasn't faking it, trying to keep me as his best friend by feigning some kind of interest. He honestly wanted me.

I pulled back the covers, and his eyes followed every motion, heating more with every second. "I hope it's okay that I borrowed your shirt."

"Yeah. More than okay."

He turned off the light as I slid into bed, pulling the covers up as my head hit the pillow.

"I'm so sorry today was a disaster."

"It wasn't." I remembered what he'd said to Bishop and scooted my back toward him until I was against his chest. His arm found its way around my waist, and I sighed in contentment as he pulled me closer.

His nose ran along the line of my neck, and I arched to give him better access. "It was."

"Maybe," I said, intertwining our fingers. "But this is worth it. This is pretty perfect."

"Yeah, you are."

His arms flexed around me and I melted. River relaxed me in a way no other man had. In so many ways this could still be just my best friend holding me, but it wasn't. Sure, it was still River, still the guy who had changed my flat tire freshman year, the guy who'd punched Troy Williams when he'd kissed me during sophomore year after I'd said no. He was the guy who had helped me with Addy, Dad, and my life in general.

He was my best friend.

But this desire to roll him over, climb on top of him, and explore every line of his body until I'd wiped away the thought of every one of those bar-bunnies he'd taken home over the years...well, that wasn't so friendly.

Was our friendship—and this blatant craving I had for him—enough to uproot my entire life?

"Avery?"

"Yeah?"

"Stop thinking about it."

"How did you—?"

"Because I know you. Stop thinking there's any expectation for this weekend and just be with me, okay? Try to forget anything else. Can you try?"

If this was really my only chance to be with him, then I had to try. I had to throw myself into this headfirst and see what was really there, because if his leaving didn't kill me, then the never knowing would.

"Yeah."

7

RIVER

*T*here was something to be said for waking up with Avery in my arms. She was soft, warm, and fit my body like she'd been made to do exactly that.

I'd already been up this morning, untangled her hair from the stubble of my beard and snuck off for a shower. Once I'd finished brushing my teeth, it was already eight thirty and she still wasn't awake.

I should have gone downstairs and found us food—I was fucking starving, but instead I crawled back into bed with her. As soon as I slid between the sheets, she rolled at me like a heat-seeking missile, using my chest as a pillow and tossing one of her thighs right across my dick.

Her best friend—I was.

A saint—I was not.

I wrapped my arm around her back, tangling it in the thick blonde strands of her hair. My chest went tight. She felt perfect wrapped around me, and it was far too easy to envision this as our life.

My free hand rested on her knee, then lightly stroked the soft skin up her thigh. I kept myself to a six-inch limit, savoring the silk of her skin under my fingers but going no higher because I knew my shirt was bunched around her waist and there was nothing between my hand and her softness besides her underwear.

When she'd walked out in my shirt last night I'd had a moment of primal possession, and it had taken everything in me not to send my hands beneath the fabric.

Even thinking about it had my dick hardening, or maybe it was the way her thigh moved against me. Either way, my body had zero issue reminding me that she was nearly naked, and so was I.

"Mmmmm," she moaned, moving even closer.

Her head shifted until her lips were pressed against my neck, and my pulse pounded beneath the innocent caress. If she honestly knew how badly I wanted her—the effort it took to keep my damn hands to myself—she never would have wanted me in bed with her.

Avery usually liked time to think things through. To examine every consequence of a possible action and then take the course she thought safest. I was damn lucky to have even stolen her away for five whole days, let alone be thinking of how easy it would be to slip my fingers inside her and bring her to orgasm before breakfast.

Not helping the hard-on situation.

She shifted again, lightly kissing my throat, and my hand tensed on her thigh, gripping the toned limb.

"Good morning." Her voice was husky from sleep and sexy as hell.

"Hey there," I said, waiting for her to understand the situation we were in.

Instead of moving away, she slid over until she rested on top of me, still pressing kisses to my neck.

"Avery." I groaned, my hands filling with the barely covered globes of her ass. Fuck me, her panties were lace.

"Hmmm?" she hummed, the vibration streaking through my nervous system and lodging in my dick. She rocked gently until I was settled directly against the heat between her thighs.

She was trying to kill me. That was the only logical explanation I could come up with. "Are you awake?"

"Yep," she said, her lips trailing down to my collarbone.

"Do you—?" I hissed when her teeth lightly grazed my skin. Damn, that felt good. "Do you know what you're doing?"

She slid farther down my body, the friction so good that my hips rolled against her. Her fingers traced the lines of my abs. "Do you mean am I aware that I'm on top of you? Kissing you?"

"Yes, that." One of my hands cupped the back of her head while the other fisted the sheet next to me.

"Do I realize that you're hard for me?" she whispered, looking up at me under her lashes with eyes so blue they rivaled the Colorado sky.

"That, too." My dick twitched in agreement.

"Yes," she said, before kissing her way down my stomach.

Holy shit. Her lips on my skin were the most exquisite torture.

"I've always wanted to do this," she said, just before tracing the lines of my abs with her tongue.

I sucked in my breath as every muscle in my body tensed. She was every fantasy I'd ever had come to life.

"Your body is incredible. I'm sure you've been told that a million times—"

Oh hell no.

I flipped her so fast that she landed with an *oomph* underneath me. Then I stretched both her arms above her head and settled in between her thighs. "Nothing mattered before you. *No one* mattered before you. Do you understand?"

She nodded, tugging her lip between her teeth.

I leaned down and sucked it free. "Speaking of incredible bodies..." My hands followed her curves, her gently tucked waist and the flare of her hips. "God, what you do to me, Avery."

Her hips rolled in my hands, and I set my mouth to her neck, loving her gasp, the way she softly said my name. Every tiny motion or sound she made drove me higher, wound me tighter.

My shirt was bunched a little higher than her waist, leaving her stomach bare to my lips. I kissed my way down her belly, letting my tongue and teeth linger where she whimpered. The skin just along her hipbone was the most sensitive, and I had her squirming under me in a matter of minutes.

"River." She moaned, her fingers in my hair, urging me on.

"I want to touch you so badly," I admitted, breathing against the band of her blue lace panties.

"So touch me."

Her words hurled me into a level of need I'd never known, intense and demanding. I wanted to roar, to mark her as mine, to let the world know that this woman deemed me good enough to put my hands on her.

I ran my hand up the inside of her thigh, my eyes locked on hers to watch for the first sign that she didn't want this. My fingers grazed the line of her underwear and then slipped under until—

Knock. Knock. Knock.

"No fucking way," I muttered. "What?" I called out as Avery giggled beneath me.

"Mr. Maldonado? I'm from the airline."

I left the warm haven of Avery's body and strode across the room, flinging the door open. "Bags?"

"Here," he said, his eyes wide. I took the bags from his hands and put them inside the door, well aware that my boxers weren't doing a damn thing to disguise my erection.

"Can you sign?" he asked.

I scrawled my signature across the paper. "Thanks for bringing them out," I said, and promptly shut the door.

Avery had sat up in bed, her hair a tousled, glorious mess, and my T-shirt pulled down to meet her thighs. I couldn't wait to strip it off her. She grinned at me and crooked her finger.

Hell yes.

Another knock at the door sounded and I cursed. "What now?" I asked as I opened the door.

Bishop was already fully dressed as he stood there with his arms crossed. He glanced down and then back up, sighing. "Play around later, little brother. We have shit to do today. We're meeting with Knox in half an hour."

"Half an hour?" Avery squealed and ran for the bathroom, dragging her small suitcase in with her.

"You seriously couldn't give me another hour?" I asked him as she shut the door.

"Consider this payback for cock-blocking me with Sarah Ganston."

"I was fourteen!" I yelled as he walked away.

"Nothing personal," he said, repeating my exact words when I'd been sent to find him for breaking curfew.

I dressed in clean clothes and then waited for Avery. We might have a full day planned, but the only thing on my agenda tonight was her.

"This is amazing," Avery whispered as we looked around the Legacy crew's clubhouse as they affectionately called it.

"Bash pulled out all the stops," Knox said as he gestured to the main room of the complex that boasted floor-to-ceiling windows and a kick-ass view of the mountains. "He wanted to make sure the Legacy crew had everything it needed."

"What about people?" Bishop asked, his eyes taking in the row of glassed-in offices on one side and the huge dining tables along the other.

The complex was massive. Double kitchens, eating areas, offices, a great room, gym, and enough rooms in the downstairs walkout level to sleep every member of the proposed twenty-two member team.

"Not going to lie, we're short," Knox admitted. "But both Emerson and Bash are working on it, and we've called every firefighting Legacy kid. So far they've all said that they're coming home, but we'll find out tomorrow."

"What's tomorrow?" Avery asked, lacing her fingers with mine.

"The council meeting," Knox answered. "We have to present them with the crew. If we have the numbers, we'll take the Legacy name."

"If we don't?" I asked.

"Ever known Bash to fail?" Knox replied.

"Ever known any of us to?" I countered.

"Exactly."

I could almost feel Avery rolling her eyes. "Okay, well let's say hell freezes over and your unfailing masculinity isn't quite enough. What then?"

Knox grinned at her. "I like you."

"Don't," I said.

Avery looked between him and me. "Are all your friends this good looking here? Because if so, then maybe Colorado really is a good idea..."

My mouth hung agape for a second while she smiled up at me. "Maybe commuting from Alaska is a good idea."

Knox laughed. "If we don't have the numbers then we'll still establish the team, it just won't be under the same banner."

"Your dads'," Avery said.

"Right."

"Either way, we're in," Bishop answered. "Even if we don't have the Legacy name, this is still their crew. Their mountain."

"Good to know," Knox said. "Now let's get to the fun part. Follow me."

He walked ahead, leading us to one of the offices with a map of Legacy on the wall. "You okay?" Avery asked quietly as we followed.

"Yeah."

"You're all tense."

I tried to relax—and failed. "The only reason I'm willing to leave Alaska and risk losing you is that it's Dad's team. It's the one they wouldn't let us restart years ago, and if we have that chance now…"

"You have to take it," she finished, looking up at me with understanding and a soft smile. "I get it. I respect you even more for it."

"But if it's not the real Legacy team, then what am I doing?"

She squeezed my hand. "Wait and see how it goes tomorrow, and then answer that question. For now…" She trailed off, looking where Bishop stood next to Knox at the map.

"What?" I asked.

"Can we just pretend for a couple of days?"

"Pretend what?" My free hand cupped her face, tilting it so she wouldn't look away.

"Pretend that this is a given? That I'll come here with you for sure?" A slight hint of panic crept into her eyes.

"Is it just pretend?" I asked softly.

"I don't want it to be, but you and I know it's so much more complicated than we're willing to admit."

I kissed her, letting my lips promise what terrified my heart. "Yeah. We can pretend. Maybe it will give you a better idea of what it would really be like if you opened yourself up to the possibility that life exists beyond the limits you've accepted."

She swallowed, then nodded. "Okay. Shall we?" She nodded toward the office.

I squeezed her hand in answer and then walked in with her at my side.

"You two good?" Bishop asked, his eyes narrowing in my direction.

"We're fantastic," I said, leading Avery over to the map.

"Right. So here's the fun part. Bash is beyond loaded now. He knew what it would take to relocate an entire Hotshot crew here, and once he realized it would be Legacy kids last week, well…he made a few calls to realtors."

Bishop and I locked eyes. He shrugged.

"That means you can either take the signing bonus that will cover the house you'd like to buy, or he'll sign you over one of the eleven he's already bought. Plus there's a new subdivision he's closing on."

"No shit?" I asked, stunned.

"No shit," Knox answered. "He wasn't letting anything get in the way. Of course there are barracks here, but if you're bringing your family"—he looked at Avery—"then he wants to make sure it's a smooth transition. Trust me, this money is nothing for him."

"Tech," I answered Avery's unspoken question. "He's sold a few apps and invested really well."

"Obscenely well," Knox added.

"Apparently," Avery said, her eyes huge.

"What do you say? Want to house hunt with me?" *Come on, Avery. Pretend.*

"I do," she said with a smile that rivaled the sun.

Five hours later, I'd fed her twice, showed her some of my favorite spots around town, and even walked her into the newspaper office.

Old Mr. Buchanan was still in charge, but he told her he was looking for a new reporter/editor/graphic designer.

"Small-town life," I said to her as we walked back to the Jeep Knox had lent us from the crew's new garage. The thing was brand new, and the weather was perfect for keeping the top off.

"I love it," she said, dropping her sunglasses down as she buckled in to the passenger side. "And thank you for driving by the high school. Addy wanted pictures."

"My pleasure," I told her as we pulled out onto the main street. "How is she doing?"

"She says Aunt Dawn has everything under control. Then again, I'm pretty sure if the house was burning down she wouldn't tell me right now."

"She knows you need the break," I said. "Where's the next house?"

She gripped the paper tightly as the wind rustled it. "Six-fifteen Pine Ave."

I entered it into the GPS and we turned left, heading for the edge of town. "I'm not sure where that is."

"Has a lot changed since you left?"

"There's more here. They'd finished a lot of the rebuild before I left for Alaska, but there's been some growth, too. I bet we're up to four thousand people by now."

"It's beautiful," she said, her eyes on the mountains around us as we left the town limits.

"What did you think about the first six houses we saw?"

"They're nice. Not exactly what I picture you in—us in," she corrected. "A little trendy, a little too close to each other."

"Agreed. I want an easy commute to the clubhouse, but I think Alaska spoiled me. I like being away from people."

"Me, too."

We followed the road deeper into the mountains until we were a good three miles outside of town. "Pine," I said, turning onto a dirt road.

"Much more your speed," she joked, reaching over to rub the back of my neck.

The road took us another mile before a house appeared on the left side of the road. "Wow," Avery sighed.

Wow, indeed. We made our way up the lengthy driveway and parked. It was log-cabin style, similar to my house back in Alaska but bigger.

"He said it was new construction," I told her as we got out of the Jeep. "Landscaping isn't finished."

She looked around the front yard. "You'd have to put in some beds there. I could plant some gorgeous flowers. The tall kind that would bring color up to the porch level."

I intertwined our fingers as we took the steps up to the porch. "Rocking chairs?" I asked.

She shook her head. "A swing."

"A swing," I agreed as I punched the code into the lock box. It popped open and I turned the handle. Then, before I could stop to think, I swung Avery up into my arms, her weight slight against my chest.

"River!" She laughed. "We're not married."

"Pretend, remember?"

She looped her arms around my neck as I carried her inside. "Wow," she said.

"You already said that," I told her as we both took it in.

"I might say it about twelve more times."

The entry and great room were open to the second floor, where there was a walkway that connected one suite of rooms to the others above us. There were more windows than walls, all looking out over the mountain range and forest.

"It's like we're the only ones on the planet," she said as I set her down. We walked over the hardwood floors of what was staged as the living room, to take in the views from the windows and sliding door to the deck.

"Want to explore?"

She nodded in excitement and took off. As was par for the course in my life, all I could do was follow her.

There was a gourmet kitchen with full appliances, a dining room, a full, finished walk-out basement, and that was before we headed upstairs. The entire house had been staged to sell, and even though the furniture wasn't exactly my style, the space was.

"Wow," Avery said again as we walked into the master bedroom. It was separated from the other three by the bridge we'd passed under downstairs. There was a bed against the far wall, two walk-in closets, a giant master bath, and an entire wall of windows that looked over the mountains, mirroring the down-stairs. A door led out to a private balcony, and we stepped onto it, both leaning against the railing that held us three stories up.

"I've never seen something so beautiful," she said, tucking the stray strands of her topknot behind her ears.

"Me either," I said, never looking away from her. She was still my Avery, but here, she felt freer, less burdened. I couldn't help but wonder how she would bloom if she were allowed the freedom to define who she was without others telling her.

"I can see it," she said softly, turning to face me.

"See what?" I was desperate to know how she envisioned life, what this house, this place looked like through her eyes, because all I saw was her.

"I can see living here. I could work at the newspaper office, and Addy could go to the high school. I see the fresh start as clearly as I can smell the new paint, and it's…"

"Scary?" I offered.

"Beautiful. It's such a beautiful picture. I can see you here, cooking in that kitchen, waking me up in the mornings with soft kisses."

"That's exactly what I want," I said.

"This house is you. You should take it." Her profile was framed by the sun-kissed strands of blonde in the afternoon light as she looked out over the sizeable backyard that ended in forest—trees and the mountains I loved almost as much as I loved her.

"This house could be us," I said, taking her hand. "I want you here, sleeping in that bedroom. Kissing me in the kitchen, racked out on the couch while we binge-watch something awful on Netflix. I want to explore these mountains with you, talk to you, laugh with you, make love to you." I brought her fingers to my mouth, kissing each one as her lips parted. "I want to make a life with you here. It's not just about leaving my best friend behind, it's about what we have between us—what we can be if we just give this a chance."

My chest tightened as I waited for her to respond, her eyes moving between mine and the landscape. I'd been so careful with her these last seven years, cautious with my feelings and how much I let her know. But laying it all out on the line was both freeing and terrifying.

I'd rather be at a fire. At least those were the flames I knew how to battle. I'd let Avery burn me if she wanted.

"It's a beautiful dream," she said softly.

"It can be reality." *Don't give up, Avery.*

She sighed. "And Addy?"

"You are under no obligation to live with me. You know that. But there's plenty of room here. I want nothing more than to wake up next to you every day, and the bedroom down the hall on the left has that great view I think she'd like."

Her eyes swam with tears. "You'd do that? Live with Adeline?"

"Adeline is pretty much my little sister, too. I have no problem helping you raise her. You've done a damn good job already, and I'd love to ease some of that. Besides, the room at the end is a three-story drop, so it's the hardest for a boy to sneak in."

She laughed, two tears racing down her face. "I don't know what to say."

I brushed the tears away with my thumbs. "Say yes. Say you'll make the crazy choice to come with me. Say you'll jump with me. For once, let's do something reckless."

"How can you be so sure we'd work out?"

The fear in her eyes might have given me pause if not for that tiny glimmer of hope I saw there, and that was what I latched onto. "Because you're already my longest relationship. You've always been the woman I've put before everyone else. I would never hurt you, never betray you, never stray from your body if I knew you felt the same."

"How do you feel?" she whispered, opening the door I'd done my damndest to keep shut all these years.

"Avery, don't you realize that I'm completely, madly, whole-heartedly in love with you?" I didn't wait for her answer, simply sealed my mouth over hers and showed her that I meant every single word.

8

AVERY

*H*is tongue consumed my mouth the way his words invaded my soul—completely and without apology.

His confession had done what I thought was impossible and brought down every last one of my defenses against him. This wasn't some fling—this was River. *My* River.

God, could the man kiss. It was a blatant, carnal exploration that had me arching against him, reaching for his head to hold him closer. He grasped me under my ass, lifting me easily, and my legs wrapped around his waist.

He brought us into the bedroom and headed for the massive four-poster bed that took up the center of the room, never once breaking the kiss or pausing. He lowered us to the mattress, and my senses ignited. The feel of the fur coverlet beneath me combined with River's taste, his scent, the weight of him as he rested between my thighs all merged together to awaken every nerve ending. The need that had pulsed within me that morning came back tenfold, demanding appeasement.

He kissed me deeper, with care and carefully checked passion. I felt his restraint in the tension of his arms, the flex of his fingers. He wanted me, but he wasn't going to do anything I wasn't fully ready for. The knowledge was heady, relaxing and inflaming all in the same moment because I knew he would give me whatever I wanted.

And he loved me.

Sweetness filled my chest and expanded outward, lingering in my limbs until his hands stroked up my rib cage, and then desire overpowered it.

I stretched my arms above my head, silently urging him to take off my shirt.

"Are you sure?" he asked.

"I want your hands on me," I whispered against his mouth, gently tugging on his lower lip with my teeth. "Here. Now."

This would be his home. I had zero doubt. For this moment, it was mine, too, because he was here. No matter what happened with us in the coming months, I wanted this with him. I wanted him to have a piece of me here even if it was only in memory.

My blue shirt came off with little fuss, and then River sucked in his breath. "Incredible," he whispered as he framed my lace-cupped breasts with his hands. His mouth collided with mine, a new edge taking over.

His thumbs grazed my hardened nipples through the lace, and I pushed into his hands, needing more.

His hand slipped beneath my back as I arched, and with a simple flick of his fingers, my bra was undone. With a motion of my arms, it found its way to the floor, and then his mouth was on me, drawing my nipple into his mouth.

"River!" I cried out as he worked the sensitive flesh. My thighs restlessly rubbed against him. I'd never been so turned on from a few touches, never been so desperate to get a man naked before...but I'd never been with River.

"Off," I demanded, yanking the fabric of his shirt.

He sat back on his heels with a wicked grin. "Your wish is my command," he said, gathering the shirt by the neck and pulling it off in one smooth motion.

My brain didn't have words for him—for the cut of his muscles, the deep tan of his warm skin, the desire darkening his eyes. He was the definition of sex, and for right now he was mine.

I kicked off my flip-flops as he stretched out over me again, leaning his weight to the side so he didn't crush me. "You are exquisite," he said, running his mouth along the underside of my jaw.

Chills raced down my body, my hips rocking involuntarily.

"So fucking sexy and finally *mine*." His words echoed my thoughts as he kissed me again, robbing me of every thought beyond his body and the magic he spun around mine. If I was this lost after a few kisses, how would I feel when he—

"River!" I gasped as his fingers slid past the waistband of my shorts.

"Tell me no," he whispered as those fingers reached my panties.

"But then you'd stop," I said, my hips moving to meet him.

"That is the rule, yes."

His hand paused just above where I needed him the most, where a dull throb had begun.

"Don't stop," I told him as my hands threaded through his hair. I loved the silky texture, the way it slid through my fingers.

"Avery." My name was a prayer on his lips as his fingers parted me and brushed my clit.

I cried out, my hips moving, my back arching, my fingers tightening their hold.

His breath stuttered in his chest. "God, if you only knew how many times I fantasized about this." He circled my clit again, then lightly rolled it.

I whimpered and kissed him as one of my hands dug into the muscles of his shoulder. "How does it live up to the fantasy?" I asked, barely able to hold on to a thought as he pressed down on me. Pleasure shot through me like electricity, tension coiling in my belly. The space was almost too tight, but he slid one finger inside me and my back came off the bed.

"There's no comparison. You're hotter, wetter..." He slipped his hand free of my shorts, then—*holy shit*—licked the finger he'd had inside me. "Sweeter than I ever imagined."

"More." It was the only word I could say because it was the only thing I wanted. I'd had sex before—I wasn't a nun—but I'd never felt this driving need, this utter desperation for someone.

He kissed his way down my stomach, then flicked open the button of my shorts and slid them over my ass and down my legs. "These have to go, too," he said, and my panties followed.

There was no shyness, no awkwardness as he looked me over like he needed to memorize this moment. The need in his eyes was enough to make me feel like a wanton goddess. His hands started at my breasts, squeezing with just the right amount of pressure, then slid down my curves, over the seam of my thighs until they reached under my ass.

He didn't look away as he brought his mouth to my core. I screamed as he licked me, sucked at me, made love to me with his fingers and then his tongue. My mind lost all control of my body as he worshipped me. I rocked against his face, loving the scrape of his stubble against my inner thighs. My hands fisted in the sheets, then his hair, anything I could grip onto as I shamelessly reveled in every sensation skyrocketing through me.

He laved at me until my body grew so tense that I could barely stand it, my need for release pounding at me. It was so damn good, the pleasure nearly unbearable until I fractured into a thousand pieces of light, his name the only word on my tongue.

His lips made their way up my body, over my navel, between my breasts, until they found mine with a surprisingly tender kiss. "God, I love that," he moaned.

"Which part?" My smile was weak as I struggled to find my breath.

"All of it. Your reactions, your taste, the way you say my name. God, especially that."

"River," I whispered and kissed his neck.

He groaned. "Yeah, that."

"River," I said again, my hands exploring the glorious muscles of his back. His skin felt like warm satin draped over knotted steel. He gasped as my fingers traced the fuck-me lines that led to his shorts. "Take these off."

A few quick motions and he was naked, his erection hot and heavy where it rested along my thigh.

"Are you sure?" he asked, looking deeply into my eyes, his thumb stroking over my lower lip.

"Yes. I want you to be mine," I answered, then kissed his thumb.

"I'm already yours in every possible way." He kissed me, reigniting the flame I was sure my orgasm had doused.

A tear of foil, and we were protected.

He picked me up easily, flipping us so that I straddled his thighs as he sat. He gave me the precious gift of control, and I reveled in the ability I had to drive him wild. I ran my hand along his length, wishing I'd taken the time earlier to taste him.

He cradled my face in his hands as I raised up on my knees and guided him to my entrance. Eyes locked, breaths ragged, hearts hammering, I lowered myself slowly, taking him inside me inch by exquisite inch. He swallowed my cry with a deep kiss, and we were joined in every possible way. My flesh stretched to accommodate him, and he was utterly still as I adjusted to him.

But then still wasn't enough. Not when he was this full, this hard inside me.

His hands kneaded my hips as I began to move, his grip digging into my flesh as I rode him. "You feel. So. Perfect," I said between glides.

"We," he corrected, kissing my neck. "*We* feel perfect."

And we were. It didn't feel like sex—more like fulfilling the union our bodies demanded because our souls had always had it. The lines of his face grew taut as he concentrated on our movements, sweat making our skin slippery as we rocked against each other, pleasure streaking through me with each motion.

His hand shifted from my thigh to strum his thumb over my clit, the nerves hypersensitive. "You don't..." I gasped as he pressed, then circled again. I tried to gather my thoughts to speak again. "You don't have to...I don't think I can..."

"Yes you can," he said, his breath warm in my ear. His free hand reached for my ponytail, wrapping it around as he gently tugged my head back. His mouth attacked my neck, licking and sucking every sensitive place. "I have seven years of fantasies, Avery. Seven years of imagining the way you'd scream my name, how tight you'd grip me as I slid into you. Seven years of waiting to feel you come around me. I have more than enough to get you there again."

I groaned, already feeling that tension starting to ravel. He shifted our angle so he could stroke deeper, our bodies undulating in perfect rhythm. It was as if we'd been making love for years, already so in tune, in sync.

"I love you." He groaned. "I'm never going to get enough of this —never going to get enough of you."

Yes, more. I moved faster, until my world was a blur of sensation and River—his breath, his body, his scent, his heart. My orgasm built until I was ready to splinter. "River," I begged.

"Yes," he hissed, then brought his mouth to mine. A few deft movements of his fingers and I came apart, my cry swallowed by his kiss.

The moment I started to sag over him, he turned, putting me on my back. Our kiss deep, he drove into me, pounding out a rhythm that had me keening, my orgasm kicking back aftershocks.

He yelled my name as he came, his muscles straining above me, and through the haze of my pleasure I could think of nothing more than how beautiful he was.

A salty kiss later, he collapsed, rolling us to the side.

Our breathing was ragged as we stared at each other. "I think we might be pretty good at that," I said.

He grinned, and my heart clenched, screaming out an emotion I couldn't—wouldn't—name.

"Yeah, but I think there might be room for improvement with practice."

"Lots of practice," I nodded.

"As much as you can handle," he promised, kissing my nose. Then all traces of laughter faded. "That was... I don't have words for it. Perfect isn't enough."

Earth shattering. Mind blowing. "Perfect is just about right."

He kissed me, holding me like I was infinitely precious to him.

"Hello? River?" A female voice came from downstairs.

We scrambled for clothes, throwing them on while he called out, "Just a minute!"

I tripped trying to put on my flip-flop, River barely catching me before I tumbled to the ground.

"All I wanted was—"

"Perfection," I said, kissing him lightly once we were right. "We've got it. Now let's see who that is."

We walked hand-in-hand down the stairs to find a petite, curvy blonde in the kitchen examining the refrigerator. She turned when she heard us, her green eyes wide with joy. "Oh my God!"

"Harper?" River asked.

By the way she jumped into his hug, I guessed she was.

He set her down and she turned to me, enveloping me in the same warm hug. "You must be Avery!" She pulled back and smiled. "Bishop said you two are pretty much fated for the diner wall. I'm Harper. Ryker's sister."

"Diner wall?" I asked as River slid me under his arm. "Ryker?"

River kissed the top of my head. "You haven't met Ryker yet. He's on a fire with Bash right now. They're Bishop's age, but I graduated with Harper. And the town has a little tradition where we carve our names into the diner wall when we're ready to declare undying love."

My heart melted. "That might be the sweetest thing I've ever heard."

Harper sighed. "It really is. Until there's a divorce or an affair and you see some crazed wife hacking at the wall with a pocket knife."

River nodded. "It happens. I love seeing you, Harper, but what are you doing all the way out here?"

"Oh, well, Knox told me that the breakers weren't on out here, and when you didn't come back, they figured you might not want to stumble around in the dark if you stayed any later."

"How did you know we were at this one?" he asked.

"I didn't. I've checked four other houses," she admitted. "Anyway, the breakers are on now, if you two want to get back to"— she gestured at us—"the amazing sex you were having."

I sputtered, my eyes flying wide. "We weren't..."

She waved us off. "Your shirt is on inside out. Anyway. Ceremony is tomorrow afternoon, and then the council meeting is tomorrow night, so you two can frolic all you like."

I wanted to die. It was like that nightmare where you're caught at school with no clothes...except mine were on inside out and this was real.

"Thanks for coming out to check on us. Does anyone deliver out here?"

She tilted her head. "Magnolia's might. Should I tell Knox you'll take this one?"

"Knox, huh?" River grinned.

She turned redder than the tank top she had on. "Shut up."

River laughed, his entire chest rumbling. "Good to see not much changes around here. Has Emerson taken Bash back yet?"

"How did you know?"

"Oh, come on. Emmy and Bash are a given. Almost as much as you dancing around Knox and praying he and your brother don't notice."

She narrowed her eyes at him. "Ugh. You've been in town for all of a day." Then she looked over at me, a small smile playing over her lips. "You and I are going to be great friends. I need someone on my team against this one."

I nodded. "I think we can manage that." I liked her openness, the way she didn't beat around the bush, and I loved the way she didn't flirt with River. Then again, I'd seen how hot Knox was, and if River was right, and that's the way her world tilted, then I couldn't blame her.

"Tell Knox we'll take this one," River said. "Do you think we have the numbers for this meeting tomorrow?"

Her smile faded. "We'll have them, one way or another."

The determination on her face was the same I'd seen on River's over the years, the same Knox had shown when he'd led us on the tour of the clubhouse. There was a steel in this generation, a tenacity that I felt simply by looking at them.

I pitied anyone who stood in the way of them getting their crew back.

9

RIVER

I traced the letters on her headstone, grief wrapping around my heart, uncaring that it had been eight years since we lost her.

"Man, I miss you," I told her before looking up to where Avery stood, flowers in her arms. "She would have loved you."

"I'm a hot mess."

"You're my hot mess," I corrected her. After the handful of times I'd taken her in the last twelve hours I was pretty sure she'd have a hard time arguing that she wasn't mine.

She placed the flowers on Mom's grave as I stood, then stepped into my arms as I held them out to her. The cemetery was quiet, peaceful.

"I'm sorry you lost them both."

"I'm glad they went close to each other. Losing Dad in the fire, that was brutal, but when cancer took her a couple years later..." He shook his head. "For a long time I wondered if I was cursed. If I wasn't supposed to have anything good."

"You deserve the best," she said, her voice soft.

"It all changed when I saw you. Frustrated, ponytail a mess, fighting with the tire iron and rusted lug nuts."

"Ugh. I'd been on the side of the road for a half hour."

I brushed her hair back from her face, loving that it was down and free. "You were beautiful, and I fell in love with you in that moment."

Her lips parted. "Because I couldn't change a tire?" she whispered.

"Because you hadn't given up. There was zero chance you could have gotten those bolts off, but you weren't giving up. When I realized that you were raising Addy, caring for your dad...there wasn't a force in this world that could have stopped me from loving you."

"Why didn't you say anything?"

"You weren't ready and I was terrified. I'd lost everyone I loved except for Bishop. When the wildfire came, when Dad died, there was a part of me that shriveled, that started to expect heartache. I couldn't show it, of course. The whole town was in mourning, and there were twenty-one of us left behind without fathers. Indigo was left without a mom. In our collective grief, we weren't allowed to break down, not when there were so many eyes on us."

"River..." she whispered, holding me tighter in her support.

"Then the rebuilding began, and Mom got sick. She died the summer of my junior year, and we had the new high school open by my senior year."

"Then you and Bishop came up to Alaska."

I rested my chin on the top of her head, loving how well she fit me. "And you know the rest."

"I wish I knew how it ended."

My heart sank, knowing as much as she loved pretending, she hadn't really decided. Because as fierce as my love of this crew and my family was, hers was just as intense for hers, and she wouldn't leave her father.

In a place that had always brought me so much loss, I couldn't help but wonder if the biggest heartache was yet to come.

"Me, too, baby."

The ceremony was somber. Bishop and I took the wreath up for our father, and then placed it at the new memorial where it stood with seventeen others.

Ten years later, and I still missed him like hell.

He'd been larger than life, a force of nature. In so many ways Bishop was just like him, but the years of raising me had hardened him in ways Dad hadn't been. Where Dad was optimistic, Bishop saw the pitfalls of everything. Where Dad loved Mom with the same kind of intensity I felt for Avery, Bishop held himself away from everyone who could leave.

As I looked around at the other Legacy kids, the ones who had grown up without their dads or mom, I realized that the casualties of that day were far more reaching than the firefighters laid to rest in Aspen Cemetery.

The entire town had lost. Homes, businesses, and memories were ash by the time the fire had finished with us, but it always felt like we had lost a little more. We took our seats, and the bells rang—one for each loss, each sacrifice, each choice that had been made the day they headed up Legacy Mountain with the odds and the weather against them.

Avery took my hand, steadying me like always. I concentrated on the feeling of her fingers with mine and tried to keep the memories at bay. But the harshest ones fought through—the order for evacuation, the way he'd held us, kissed our mother. The way he'd told Bishop to keep me out of trouble while he was gone.

My resolve sharpened with each bell. The council could be afraid of the liability of having another Hotshot crew. They could deny us the Legacy name, and they could claim it was to salvage the tender hearts of this town.

But the Legacy crew had been family, and damn it, we were getting it back.

As the ceremony cleared out, the twenty-one of us stood in a line facing the monument, from the youngest kid, Violet, who had never met her father, to the oldest, Shane Winston, who'd been away at college when it happened.

Those who wouldn't be joining us on the crew—the ones who were too young or who had no interest in firefighting—left, until it was just those of us who were.

"Are you sure about this?" Bash asked, Emerson by his side. Time had turned the dark-haired, reckless guy into a hell of a stubborn man.

I looked around as we all nodded.

"They're going to fight us tooth and nail," he warned. "They don't want this. They're terrified of what could happen." He looked pointedly at our youngest members who couldn't be older than twenty.

"We're with you, Bash," Bishop answered from next to me. "They're not taking this from us."

"We're with you," we all agreed.

Avery's soft smile was forced as I looked down at her, and I sent up a fervent prayer that she would stay, because I knew in that moment there was no way I could leave.

10

AVERY

"*S*o which one is that?" I asked Harper as we looked over the packed clubhouse.

The Legacy crew had gotten their needed numbers, and the council had begrudgingly approved the team after Spencer—the only surviving member of the original team—showed up and agreed to lead them.

"That's Ryker," Harper answered. "He's my brother."

"Right," I said, trying to remember names with faces. "And the one standing next to River is Bash."

"Yup. Sebastian Vargas, but everyone's called him Bash since he was little. And Emerson is the brunette standing next to him. She's my best friend."

"Too many names," I muttered.

She laughed and took a sip of her beer. "You'll figure it out. Don't worry. The crew is a giant family. We're together a lot, so you'll learn."

If I'm here.

The longer we were here, the more I wanted to—hell, *needed* to. I loved everything about the little town, the people, the crew... and River. All I had to do was convince Dad to come, that maybe the change would be good for him, too. River was pretty much a saint to offer for Dad to live with us, but maybe he'd get to where he could live on his own...and I could have my own life.

The texts Addy had sent me said everything was under control, so maybe it was possible.

Yes. I could do it. Maybe.

"What's up, Avery?" Bishop asked as he walked over.

"Can we take a walk?" I asked him, needing a sounding board that wasn't River.

His forehead puckered. "Of course."

He helped me up and we walked out the side door of the clubhouse. I sucked in a deep lungful of air, grateful for the quiet we had outside. My lungs burned, but I was adjusting to the altitude. Kind of.

"What are you going to do?" he asked, never one to beat around the bush.

"I don't know," I answered.

"What do you want?" he asked. "Not what River wants, what your dad wants...what do *you* want?"

I thought about the last two days. The peace, the freedom, the pure happiness I felt at the possibility of a fresh start with River. "I want to be here."

"Then that's your answer."

I scoffed. "What I want and what's possible are almost never the same thing."

"Avery, if you're willing to tear up everything, move from Alaska, and build something fresh, then you've already jumped the biggest barrier. Well, that and chancing your life on River's cooking."

My lips turned up at the corners. "Okay, there's that. Do you really think I can convince my dad to come? Adeline is all for it, but it's not just me in this decision. I can't leave them any more than you'd leave River."

His face scrunched. "Eh, you know, River is a grown-ass man. If he didn't want to come here, I would have left him in Alaska. He makes his own choices. Of course, I'm glad he's here with me. If he's going to be firefighting, then I want him on my crew, but don't think for a second that I wouldn't have come without him. He deserves his own life, and you do, too."

"And what if I come here, and it doesn't work out with River?" I asked, giving voice to my biggest fear. "What if I leave everything I know behind, and come here, and we have a horrid breakup and then I lose him anyway?"

He grasped both of my shoulders and ducked to look in my eyes. "That's a risk you're going to have to take. Nothing is guaranteed, not in life and sure as hell not in love. But I can tell you that he has loved you for as long as he's known you. There is nothing he won't give you—nothing he won't do to make this work. That kind of love, the one that's rooted in a friendship as deep as you two have…that's not easy to come by. It's worth the fight. I'll tell you the same thing I told him. You guys are worth the gamble."

"Thank you," I said softly.

"Don't thank me. You have a hell of a road ahead of you. I just wish that I could be there to help you with it."

"You're not coming back with us?" My stomach dropped.

"Nah. I boxed up my shit before I left. River is going to sell my truck and send my stuff with his. Bash needs my help here. We have a ton of relocating to do, and there's not much up there for me anyway."

"I guess I thought when they told us you could have until spring…" My voice drifted off because we both knew where it was going. When Bash had gotten approval for the team to be together by spring, I figured we'd been given a reprieve. Another few months to work everything out. Time to convince my dad. Time to coordinate.

"River might take it," Bishop said. "Like I said, we make our own decisions. If he chooses to stay the winter in Alaska, then I'll support that. He doesn't have to be back until April."

"I just need time."

"I know that, and he does, too. It's just that time might not be something we have a lot of to spare right now."

The door opened behind us and River stepped out. "Hey, are you stealing my girl, or what?"

Bishop gave my shoulders one last squeeze. "Nope, she's all yours." He went for the door but turned before going in. "Remember what I said, Avery. His cooking really will kill you." He tossed a grin at River and went inside, leaving us alone.

"Asshole," River muttered.

"Are you going to take the time?" I asked. "Are you going to stay in Alaska until spring, or are you moving right now?"

His eyebrows shot high. "Well, I guess that's what you two were talking about."

"Answer, please? Because I'm kind of freaking out."

He took two steps and enveloped me in his arms, pulling me close. I rested my head on his chest, letting his familiar scent and heartbeat surround me.

"I'll do whatever you need," he said, his chin resting on the top of my head. "If you want to move now, we'll get Addy, your dad, and move. If you want to wait until spring, I'll have to come back a few times, but we can make that happen, too."

"You'd wait for me to get everything together?"

His arms tightened around me. "If I know that you're coming here, making your life with me, I'll wait forever."

I took a stuttering breath, knowing that what I was going to say would change everything. Then I looked up at him, meeting his dark eyes in the bright moonlight. "I want to come. I want to live here with you. Well, not *here*, here, but at our house *here*. I want to make this work. I'll do it."

Saying the words set my heart free in a way I'd never known. Every possibility for my future was so clear, so vibrant that I could taste it, and then River was all I could taste as he kissed me.

This was what I wanted for my life. River's kisses, his arms around me, his love. I wanted it all.

His kiss was passionate, claiming, and I found my back against the building as he pinned me between him and the wall. It didn't matter that I'd already kissed him dozens of times in the last week. Each kiss felt new, and at the same time like coming home.

"This is yours," he said, his lips brushing my ear as something cold and metal pressed into my palm.

"A key?" I asked, examining it in the pale light.

His smile could have lit the world. "I just signed for the house. This one is yours. No pressure. It's just a key."

It wasn't just a key. "I love it," I said, my hand closing so tight the ridges bit into my skin.

"I love you," he said.

My heart soared, erupted, as if by saying what I wanted, I'd finally cut loose the chains I'd tightly bound myself with. "River," I whispered, pulling him back so I could look into his eyes when I said it. "I—"

My phone sounded with Addy's ringtone. Calling wasn't in her nature, she was more of a text girl, so it had to be urgent.

"Ugh." I sighed, pulling my phone from my pocket. "One second." I swiped the phone and answered. "What's up?"

"Avery?" she sobbed.

My stomach soured and my world narrowed to the small voice on the other end. "What's wrong?" I asked her.

"It's Dad. He…" Another sob came through, and I forced oxygen through my lungs. "Aunt Dawn didn't move the meds, and he found them."

"Oh, God." I would have fallen if River's arms hadn't caught me, holding me upright. "Addy, is he…?"

"He overdosed. They have him on a ventilator and they don't know…" Her voice faded into hiccupping sobs. "Can you come home?"

I looked up into River's eyes and realized he'd heard her through the phone when he nodded. The earth shifted beneath my feet; the reality I'd been so certain of a few minutes ago disappearing as a new one took its place.

"I'm on my way."

11

RIVER

I took another sip of hospital coffee and tried to stay awake. We'd been traveling sixteen hours, having driven to Denver the night before to get the first flight out. Avery couldn't wait to fly out of Gunnison in the morning.

We'd come straight to the hospital where her dad was in the ICU, and I'd been sitting out here for at least another two hours, just hoping that she was okay in there with him.

"They say if he makes it through the night, he should be okay," Adeline said, curled into my side.

"He's a tough guy, your dad," I told her. It didn't matter what an ass he'd been; no kid deserved to lose her father this way.

"I hate him," she whispered. "Why can't he just be like other dads?"

I put my coffee down and wrapped my other arm around her. "I know, and you know what? It's not fair. But I do know that you and your sister are some of the strongest, smartest women I know, and I think that has a lot to do with what you've been through. Don't hate him, Addy. He struggles with something we can't understand."

Problem was, I hated him. I hated that the moment Avery found out he'd overdosed, she'd clammed up. She went distant. Gone were the soft looks, the warm touches. Gone were the kisses, the talks about our future. She stared out the fucking window on every airplane and responded to questions in one-word answers.

My Avery was gone in the span of a heartbeat as we'd packed, driven, flown, and arrived. It wasn't even that she'd pulled away romantically that pissed me off. It was that she'd blocked me as her best friend. She'd closed herself down and built a wall so high I'd need a damn ladder.

"Do you want me to take you home?" I asked Addy.

"No. I'm scared that if I leave…"

He won't be alive when I come back. I heard it loud and clear without her uttering a word.

"I understand."

Another hour passed before Avery walked out.

I moved to sit up straight, but she shook her head. "He's still… He's alive," she whispered as she motioned to Addy. "How long has she been asleep?"

"About a half hour," I said softly.

She nodded, taking the seat on the other side of me. Her skin was pale in gross contrast to the dark circles under her eyes. The worst part was that they were flat, giving away no hint of whatever emotion she was feeling.

"How is he?" I asked.

"Stable." She shrugged. "Aunt Dawn is a mess. I never told her how bad it really was. Figured if I could handle it on my own, why air the laundry, you know?"

I threaded our fingers and squeezed lightly. "You've done a damn fine job. Better than anyone else could have. What happened here is not your fault. It's his."

She nodded slowly, repetitively, which moved to slight rocking motions. "I should have been here."

Boom. I heard my heart hit the floor with every word. "This isn't your fault," I repeated. "You have to know that or it will eat you up."

She kept rocking, but the head nod changed to her shaking it. "I should have been here. I know to move the meds. I know what he's capable of."

"Avery," I begged.

She stood up, dropped my hand, and walked back into the ICU.

Two days later he was still alive.

I wasn't so sure about Avery. She was gaunt, quiet, and barely left his room unless the nurses told her she had to. She slept on the waiting room couches and only went home to shower.

I'd given up on trying to get her to talk to me yesterday. Avery would open up when she wanted to, and until then it was like chipping away at Fort Knox with a fucking toothpick.

So instead of sitting there for hours, waiting for her to realize I was right next to her, I started on the list Bishop had texted me.

"Friday is great," I told the moving company. "I'm just impressed you can get it done by then. Thank you."

I hung up and crossed *coordinate movers* off my to-do list as I chugged down a glass of water.

I'd already put his truck on Craigslist and had an appointment to show it to a potential buyer. Not bad for a Tuesday morning.

On the flipside, he was having the satellite installed at our new place in Colorado.

Is it ours? Is she even coming?

A knock at the door startled Zeus, but he was wagging like a puppy when I opened the door to find Avery standing there. Her hair was up in a messy knot, but it was clean, and her jeans and baseball tee were different than the outfit I'd seen her in this morning.

"Hey. You didn't have to knock."

She shrugged, preoccupied with petting Zeus. "I didn't want to barge in. Do you have a couple of minutes?" Finally, she looked up at me, but the cool, detached look in her eyes had my stomach somersaulting.

"Of course. Come on in."

She passed me in the doorway, careful not to brush against me, and my senses went on high alert, warning bells screaming in my ears. "Dad's awake," she said, crossing her arms in front of her chest. The move didn't look defensive, more like what she would do to hold herself together.

"That's great!" He was going to be okay. My relief was short-lived because when I reached for her, she stepped away. "Avery?"

She shook her head, her teeth sinking into her bottom lip momentarily. "Just stay over there. I can't think when you touch me."

"Okay," I said slowly, tucking my thumbs into the pockets of my shorts to keep my hands off her. She looked so small, defenseless, and it was ripping me apart that she didn't want me to touch her.

"He's awake and talking since this morning, right after you left, actually."

"That's good. What's wrong? This is good—no, great news. He's going to be okay. Maybe this will be a turning point for him."

She laughed, the sound bitter and empty. "He won't change. He's never going to change. And he won't go to Colorado. He refuses. Says that this whole thing was my fault for being gone, and that the minute I leave he'll do it again."

"Avery…" God, I wanted to strangle him with my bare hands. None of this was her fault, but he'd gotten it into her so young —the guilt, the obligation—until it became part of her very being.

"It wasn't even intentional, that's the kicker. He didn't take the whole bottle or anything, just upped his pain meds. But the dosage he was already on gave him an accidental overdose."

"This wasn't your fault. I will say it every minute of every day until you realize that. He's an adult. He made a choice."

"But it is my fault," she cried. "I left. I believed that someone else could care for him, and this is what happened. None of this would have happened if I'd been here—where I'm supposed to be, taking care of my family." She rubbed her hands over her bloodshot eyes, the blue even brighter than usual. "What was I thinking?"

I walked over to her, damning her instructions, and gently lifted her wrists so I could see her face. "You were thinking that you deserve happiness, too. You deserve a life, love, kids, a future that isn't all about when he decides to go off the rails."

"But I don't." Her voice was quiet, her eyes pleading for something I didn't know how to give. "Sometimes we draw the short straw. You lost your dad, then your mom. Are you telling me you wouldn't feel the same if it was them? If you had a chance to be there for them, would you leave? Or would you suck up the bitterness because it's the straw you were dealt, and just be thankful you have them around?"

The small piece of hope I'd kept cradled close screamed out its defeat and died. "You're not coming back to Colorado with me right now."

She shook her head. "I can't. Look what happened when I left him."

I took a deep, steadying breath and pulled out plan B. "Okay, then we'll spend the winter here, get him healthy, and talk about it again in the spring. By then maybe his head will be clear enough to make a better choice."

"No," she whispered. "He said he'll die in that house before he moves. It's where we all lived when Mom was alive, and that's all there is left."

"I typically draw the line at relocating an entire house, but I can make some calls," I tried to joke. I was grasping at straws as they slid through my hands.

"He's lonely. He said that I'm never there, and he's right. Between working both jobs and seeing…"

"Me," I offered, my tone tensing.

"You," she agreed softly. "With all that, I'm not around for him, and there's no one else he'll let in."

"What are you saying?" I asked, the pit in my stomach growing to black-hole proportions.

She looked up at me, the sadness of the world pouring out of her eyes, and I knew. I fucking *knew.* "You're not coming at all."

"I can't. I would never forgive myself if something happened to him."

My mind swam, trying to come up with plan C. "Okay, so I'll go seasonal. I'll work with the Legacy crew in the summer, and come back for winters. It will suck, but we can manage it."

She shook her head. "No. It wouldn't work. We'd both be miserable, and eventually you'd resent me. We'd just be prolonging the inevitable."

"Don't do this."

She tugged her wrists free and cupped my face with her hands, scratching her palms over my day's worth of stubble. "You are the most beautiful dream. What we could have had…that was another life, with another girl who could walk away from her responsibility. That girl is never going to be me. Maybe if Adeline was grown, but there's just too much here."

"I can call Bash. I'll back out of the team. There's one other guy they could call, and I'll make sure he takes the slot."

She brushed her thumb over my lower lip. "You staying won't fix anything. I'd cost you the chance to be on the Legacy crew."

"I don't care. Nothing matters without you."

Her hands fell from my face, and I realized that I was wrong. I wasn't grasping at straws—I was desperately clutching at her, and she fell through my fingers like running water, impossible to hold and yet even harder to whisk away in its entirety. She'd already soaked into my soul.

"I can't be with you, River. Not now. Not ever. I can't go, and you can't stay. Our dream was beautiful—the happiest few days of my life—but it's time to wake up. I'm not a child. I can't do selfish things, and not everyone gets the fairy tale."

"You are my fairy tale," I argued. "You are the only woman I have ever loved. The only woman I *will ever* love, and I'm not giving up that easily."

"I'm not giving you a choice!" she yelled, backing away from me. The lack of physical contact felt like having a limb severed. My nerves screamed to have her back. "God, can't you see? I'm still the girl with the goddamned rusted lug nuts on the flat tire. I'm not going to back down. I'm not going to leave him. That's not what good people do!"

I raked my hands down my face. "So what am I supposed to do? Leave you because you're honorable? Because you stepped up to do what no one else would? Do you expect me to be less than the man you know by walking away?"

She shook her head, two crystal tears streaking down her cheeks. "No. I expect you to do what you need to for *your* family. Go to Colorado. Become what you were destined to be. Live in that house and be happy, River. Just be happy!"

"I can't be happy without you! Is that seriously what you think of me? That I can move, start over? Forget that you exist? You're in every single breath I take, every thought I have. I'm not leaving you here to carry this by yourself. To raise Addy, to take care of your dad, to work yourself to death. That's not in my nature."

"It's not your choice to make," she said, furiously wiping her tears away. "Whether or not you're still here, we're over. I won't sit by and watch you resent me, watch you kiss that picture every time you come home from a fire. That will kill me far more than knowing you're happy somewhere else...with someone else."

Pure, white-hot rage choked me, and I had to swallow a couple times before I was under control. "If you think you're that easily replaceable, then you never really knew me."

"We only had a few days," she said quietly.

"We had seven fucking years."

"And they're over. We're over."

"Avery..."

"What's your solution, River? What happens if you stay here and Bishop is killed on a fire? You wouldn't ever recover from that. The guilt alone would destroy you. What if I go there and my dad dies because I wasn't here to take care of him? I'm his daughter. His flesh and bone. I owe this to my mother. I promised her, and as much as I—" My heart stopped as she sucked in a breath, closing her eyes for a moment. "As much as I care for you, it would turn to hate for putting me in that position where I have to choose to abandon my family to be with you."

Hate. The word drove a knife through my chest, and as sure as if it was a physical wound, my heart bled out on my hardwood floor. "You're really ending this."

"I don't have a choice."

I shook my head. "No, you have *all* the choices, you're just refusing to make them. I'm not saying they're easy choices, but at least you have them. Me, on the other hand, I get to stand here while you shred me because you're not willing to take a fucking chance!"

"There's no chance to take! This is a certainty."

"You have no idea what could happen over the winter. None. You're letting him manipulate you, as usual. As your best friend, I stood by and watched you put yourself last over and over. But as the man who loves you, openly and out loud, I can't stand to watch you do this to yourself."

"I'm telling you not to watch. I'm telling you to go."

"It's bullshit that you think you get to make that choice for me!"

"You're like this kid in a car, speeding toward the cliff, knowing that it's coming but refusing to turn, or just *stop*."

"And you're too scared of the cliff to find another way," I threw back.

"Do you realize what happens when you jump off a damn cliff? You fall. You die. The ground crushes you."

"Or maybe you fly. Damn it, Avery, why do you make it so hard to love you? Why can't you just let me love you?"

She looked like I'd slapped her, those eyes huge and pooling with tears as we stood facing each other, the only sound in the room the pounding of my heart, the rush of blood through my ears.

"I never wanted it to end this way," she whispered.

"Yeah, well, I never wanted it to end."

"I'm so sorry," she whispered.

"That makes two of us."

She nodded and walked to the door, pausing at the frame to look back. "Goodbye, River."

I fought against every one of my instincts that demanded I go after her and kiss some sense into her, force her into seeing that we could make it. No matter how imperfect our circumstances, we were perfect for each other. But I was done forcing her to see the possibilities. This was her choice.

Every muscle in my body locked as I spoke the words she wanted.

"Bye, Avery."

The sound of the door closing reverberated though every cell of my body. Only then did I say the words I needed.

"I love you."

The future I'd planned, dreamed of, yearned for disintegrated in front of me. My heart shattered with the glass I threw against the wall, water dripping down the wall and soaking into the paint.

12

AVERY

"I'm the one in the hospital, but you're the one who looks like shit," Dad said as I walked into his room.

"Get off her case, Jim," Aunt Dawn said from the chair next to his bed. "Honey, are you okay?"

"I'm fine," I replied, giving the same answer I had for the last three days since I'd left River.

I said it to everyone at work when they asked about how red my eyes were. I said it to Addy when she caught me staring off into space, thinking about him. I said it to myself every time I felt my walls crumble and the *not-fine* emotions surface.

"Fine or not, you look like crap," Dad repeated, sitting up in bed with a wince. "I wish they hadn't lowered my meds."

"You have to be able to function," I said. "Besides, with the new physical therapy, maybe we can wean you off them."

"I'm not seeing a physical therapist," he grumbled.

"Yeah, why bother with something that might help you?" I snapped. "Why not just up the pain meds until we're here again?"

"Watch your tone!" He seethed. "Your mother would be ashamed!"

My mouth snapped shut, heat flushing my face. She had handled him with more grace than I ever would manage...and she had died for it.

"Jim," Aunt Dawn warned. "Avery didn't put you in this hospital. You did that yourself."

Before he could snap back at her, the doctor came in to discharge Dad. I stared out the window in the direction of River's house, wondering what he was doing, how mad at me he still was.

Did I make a mistake? I shut that line of thinking down before it could destroy me. There hadn't been a choice to make. I had to set him free before we destroyed each other.

Too late.

I listened as the doctor gave the discharge instructions to my aunt. The pain meds he was allowed, the therapist he needed to see. It should have been me the doctor gave the instructions to. After all, I was the one who was responsible for Dad. But this doc wouldn't know that. In appearances, it made sense that the fifty-ish woman was caring for the fifty-ish man.

Not the twenty-five year old.

A little over an hour later, we had Dad settled back on the living room couch. "Give me the remote," he demanded when Aunt Dawn went to grab his bag from the car.

I handed it over without a word, too tired to fight with him over manners.

"Give me one of those white pills."

"No, it's not time yet," I told him, removing the medication.

"You're not the adult here!" he screamed.

"Of course I am!" I fired back. "That's what you made me! You want to be the grown-up then you have to act like it."

I put the meds in the small breadbox on top of the refrigerator, gripped the counter, and leaned over, trying to get a breath. Everything suddenly felt stifling, as if the walls of my life were suddenly moving closer—like I was stuck in that trash compactor on Star Wars.

But I'd let my Han Solo walk away.

Gasping for air, I stumbled to the front door, grabbing my car keys on the way out. I needed to see him. Even if it was only for a second. Even if he told me to go the hell away, I needed him.

"Avery?" Aunt Dawn bumped into me on the bottom steps. "Are you okay?"

"I'm fine," I replied automatically, sucking in the clean, sweet air. "I just need to run an errand. Do you think you could stay with him?"

"Of course."

"Thank you," I said, nearly running to my car.

"Honey," she called out. "You don't have to do this—take care of him on your own. I didn't know how bad it was, you were that good at caring for him. But I'm here now. I'm not leaving you to do this on your own, do you understand?"

"He's my father," I said with a shrug.

"He's my little brother. He was my responsibility long before he was yours. Don't you let your father's actions stop you from living your life. Do you understand me? I won't stand for it, and neither would your mother."

I nodded, unable to think of anything to say, then slid behind the wheel. She waved before disappearing into the house, and I backed out of our driveway, more than desperate to get to River.

Maybe River was right. Maybe if I had Aunt Dawn to push Dad, he'd get better—at least well enough to move to Colorado. Maybe all he needed was the winter.

Maybe there was something at the cliff's edge.

I sped across the back roads toward River's house. I'd never gone this long without talking to him unless he was on a fire, and we'd never been in a fight this severe, but I knew it could be fixed.

He was River. I was Avery. It was as simple as that.

I pulled into his driveway and killed the ignition, running for the house before I heard the car door fully shut behind me. Zeus wasn't barking, so maybe they were out for a run.

I fumbled with my keys, pulling out the small bronze one he'd given me years ago, and opened the door.

"River? I used my—" The air rushed from my lungs as I looked into his perfectly clean, perfectly empty house. "Key."

Everything was gone. The furniture. The dishes. Zeus's bowls. The house I loved had been transformed into an empty shell. Somehow I got my feet to move, to carry me to the kitchen counter where there was a stack of papers. There was a listing agreement and a note to Mindy Ruiz, a local realtor.

Hey, Mindy,

Here's the listing agreement. Sorry I had to leave so fast. It just made sense to send all my stuff with Bishop's. You'll find his listing agreement under mine. If you need anything else, I'll forward my new number from Colorado. All the keys are here except one. Avery Claire has it. Let her keep it. I'll pay to have the locks redone when you find new buyers.

Thanks,

River Maldonado

He was gone. Really and truly gone. *Because I told him to go.*

My back hit the cabinet and I fell to the ground. Hugging my knees to my chest, I finally succumbed to my emotions, letting them out of the cage I'd locked them in.

I loved him. I'd always thought if I didn't acknowledge that fact, it wouldn't have the power to hurt me, but I was pulverized all the same. Whether or not I'd told him, or even myself, didn't matter. The love was still there, and the ache was pure agony.

I'd had him. Touched him. Loved him. I'd held his heart in my hands and then thrown it back at him.

My sobs echoed through the empty house until my body ran out of tears. By the time I left, it was dark—and I was broken.

"I want to move to Colorado," Adeline said as she helped me load the dishwasher.

"They have some really great colleges there. Why don't we do some research? It's only five years away." I slipped another glass into the top rack.

"Because I want to go *now.*"

My stomach tightened. "Yeah, well, we can't. Look what happened when I left last time." It had been three weeks since he'd overdosed. Two since River moved to Colorado.

One since he posted a photo of his new house on Instagram with the caption that he was home in Legacy for good.

"Where's that beer?" Dad called out from the living room.

"That was his choice," Addy whispered.

I grabbed a clean glass from the cabinet, filled it with ice and water, and walked out of the kitchen without replying. How could she understand? She was only thirteen. I'd been two years older when Mom died, and even then I hadn't fully understood.

"Here we go," I said to Dad as I put the glass within his reach on the coffee table.

"What is that bullshit?" he spat.

"That is water. Doc said no booze, remember?" I counted to ten in my head, reminding myself that he was an addict.

"I don't give a fuck what that doctor said. Get me a beer before your aunt Dawn gets back from the store."

"No," I said with a shake of my head.

"Girl!" he yelled, and I heard Adeline go silent in the kitchen. The water was running, but no dishes clanked.

"I didn't give up everything good in my life just so you could sit there and drink yourself to death," I said calmly.

"Get me the goddamned beer! Gave up everything good? What would you know? Because you broke up with a boy who you dated for all of five seconds? I lost your mother!"

"I did, too!" I yelled. "You aren't the only one who lost her!"

Something went sailing past my head and smashed against the wall. I spun to see water running down the wall into a puddle of ice and smashed glass.

"Clean that up!" he yelled.

"Clean it up yourself," I snapped and walked away.

My chest heaved as I ran outside, gasping for the clean air as I sat on the front steps, my head in my hands. He'd fucking thrown a glass at me. What was next? Would he hit me? Would he hit Addy?

The doc had warned us that he would get worse before he got better. That weaning him down from the pain meds wasn't going to be pleasant, but this was horrid. Maybe I needed to send Addy to a friend's house for the next month or so.

The door opened and shut behind me and Adeline joined me on the step. "I want to move *now*."

"I know," I said, putting my arm around her. "But we can't just leave him."

"We wouldn't be. Aunt Dawn is here. She's already offered to take care of him, and let's face it—she's the only one he's remotely scared of."

"That's true, but he's our dad."

"He's never going to forgive us for Mom dying," she whispered.

I wanted to tell her that wasn't true, but I'd made a promise to never lie to her, so I stayed silent.

"Avery?"

"Yeah?"

"I did something."

My stomach clenched. "Okay. What did you do?"

"You know my savings?"

"I do." She hated that I made her save half of every birthday gift from our extended family.

"I spent it yesterday."

Before I could flip out on her that she'd need that when she went to college, she unfolded a paper from her back pocket and handed it to me.

Doing my best to keep my hands from trembling, I opened it up. Then my jaw dropped. "You want me to be your legal guardian?"

She nodded. "There's nothing left for us here, Avery. You're already more of a parent than he is. This would just make it possible…"

"For us to move to Colorado without him," I whispered.

"For us to be free."

I hugged her to me, and for the first time in my life, I considered leaving him behind.

∼

"You're sure you're okay to get him to his appointment?" I asked Aunt Dawn.

"Yes, Avery. You go to work. Maybe stay out late? Go see a movie?"

It had been a month since River left, and I still hadn't ventured out for more than work, groceries, or getting Adeline to school. Just like River's house had become nothing more than a shell when he left, I was hollowing out on the inside without him.

I stalked his Instagram like a mad woman, savoring the pictures he took of Legacy, of the views from his run, or the deck. *Where he told me that he loved me.*

As much as those pictures hurt, it was nothing compared to the pain that ripped me in two when his house here sold.

As I reached for a pre-work snack, I saw a pamphlet on the counter. "LaVerna Lodge. What's this?"

"That's an extended rehab center," Aunt Dawn said slowly. "I wanted to talk to you about it later. He's not getting any better with how we're doing things, and I thought maybe he needed a little more structure. A firmer hand."

He hadn't had another violent outburst, but he hadn't cleaned up the glass he'd broken, either. He'd been careful with his words, especially when Aunt Dawn was around. Maybe Addy was right and I wasn't what he needed to get healthy. "You think this is what he needs?"

She covered my hand with hers. "I do. I have the money, you don't have to worry about that. But I think you both need to go. Him to the recovery center and you to that man you love so desperately."

A lump formed in my throat. "That ship sailed."

"Chase it down," she said softly. "You have your whole life ahead of you. Let your dad get healthy. Right now he doesn't deserve you, and there comes a point where you need to recognize that he's not your responsibility, no matter how much you claim otherwise."

Never tell, Avery. You can never tell. Mom's words came back to me as I glanced at the pamphlet. "He'll never agree. His addiction…it was something he would never let on in the public."

"Now that, my dear, is a ship that's sailed. The ambulance and hospital stay outed him pretty damn loudly. I honestly don't know why you didn't come to me earlier."

"I…he…" I stuttered. "I did it for Mom, because I was scared that if I left, or I brought attention to it, the system would take Addy. She was so little, and I was still in high school."

"You're not anymore. You'd be more than fit as a guardian…if you wanted to be. I'm here. I'm not going anywhere, and if you want to go, I can take care of Adeline. Either way, we really need to get him into treatment."

I nodded. She was right about everything. The same fear that had me covering his ass all these years didn't come into play anymore. "Maybe I can talk to him about it." A quick glance at my phone told me I had thirty minutes before I needed to leave. "Let me get dressed for work, first."

Ten minutes later, I walked toward the living room but paused just outside the door when I heard Aunt Dawn talking with Adeline, and I shamelessly eavesdropped.

"They have a great pre-law program, and the campus is gorgeous," Addy said.

"I'm sure it is, baby. I'm so proud of you for thinking ahead. Have you looked anywhere local?" Aunt Dawn asked.

Dad struggled to sit up, and Aunt Dawn helped him, propping a pillow behind his back.

Addy licked her lips nervously, her eyes darting toward Dad before answering. "Not really. I think I belong there. Colorado just kind of calls to me."

I smiled at the wistfulness in her voice, the way her world seemed so open, everything possible. She had the determination to do it, too. Once Adeline put her mind to something, it was pretty much a done deal.

"What about Avery?" Dad asked, turning his eyes soft in a way I had only seen when he wanted something.

Chills raced down my spine.

"What about her?" Adeline asked carefully. "She loves Colorado."

"She does, but she won't leave here. This is her home—your home, too, but I understand you wanting to stretch your wings. Our little town isn't for everyone, is it?"

"No," she said quietly, looking at her hands.

"I guess…" He shook his head, and I leaned closer.

"What?" she asked in a small voice.

"I just guess I never saw you as being the kind of girl who would abandon her family."

Oh, hell no.

"Oh, that's not what she'd be doing—" Aunt Dawn argued, but the damage was done.

Addy's shoulders slumped. "I guess I'd never thought of it that way."

"I bet Avery has," he said, reaching for her hand. "I don't know how she'd get by without you."

Every time he'd used those exact words on me flooded my head, the memories bringing with them the kind of cold rage I hadn't felt since the night Mom died.

It wasn't about family for him. If it was, he'd be content that I was here to take care of him and he would have eventually let Adeline go. No, it was about control.

And I was taking it back.

I walked to the hall table and calmly took out Adeline's folded paper, then grabbed a pen and went back to the living room, Aunt Dawn following me with her head tilted.

"Avery?"

I ignored her and made a beeline straight for my father. "Addy, move," I instructed her.

She jumped, moving out of the way. I didn't look at her, instead I focused completely on the man who'd blamed me for his misery since I was fifteen.

"Sign it," I said, handing him the paper and pen.

"What?" he scoffed, opening the paper. "Like hell am I signing this."

"You'll sign it," I told him. "I'm taking Adeline to Colorado. She's going to have a life. She's going to finish out a real childhood and then be whatever the hell she wants when she grows up. She's not staying here under your thumb so you can guilt her into spending her life in this house. I refuse. Sign the goddamned paper."

"Have you lost your mind, girl?" he spat at me. "She's my child. You want to leave? Go. No one's stopping you. Good riddance. But she stays." He pointed the pen at Adeline.

I sat in the chair, leaning close to him so only he could hear me. "You sign that paper, or I will tell her why our mother is really dead." He tensed. "You were high while you were driving. You see, you can play off your addiction as the result of that crash and get all the sympathy, but I'm old enough to remember. We were at Grandma's because Mom needed to dry you out before your work buddies realized what you'd become. I know because I wasn't a kid when it happened, Dad. I heard her on the phone. I knew what drug paraphernalia looked like."

"You wouldn't," he whispered, his eyes wide with panic.

"I would. For Adeline, I would. You can blame us for being born all you want, but you were an addict way before that accident. And I know that the only reason you weren't put in jail was because you were on the force and your buddy figured losing Mom would change you. He didn't want to take you away from us."

"Avery…"

"I hated you, but I was also so grateful just to have you alive."

"Please don't…"

"But I don't feel that way anymore. I have no problem writing a huge article about it for the paper. Sure, maybe no one will believe me, but chances are they all will—including Adeline. Sign the paper, Dad. Free her. Get healthy. Then come find us, and we'll see if we can ever repair what you've systematically destroyed. Until then… Sign. The. Fucking. Paper."

A simple movement of his wrist, and Adeline was free.

And so was I.

13

RIVER

*M*y heart pounded as I finished my run. When the hell was I finally going to adjust to this altitude? I'd been running every day for the last five weeks and I still felt like I needed a lung transplant after four miles.

"It's embarrassing, Zeus," I said as we stretched out near the steps.

He looked up at me with an exasperated expression and laid down while I worked out my quads. I glanced over at the flower beds I'd put in last weekend and wondered what Avery would have planted.

Would she have wanted one around the mail box I'd just put in? Did it even fucking matter? I closed my eyes against the onslaught of pain I knew was coming. Every time I thought about her was followed by an exquisite ache somewhere in the vicinity of where my heart used to be.

I clicked my tongue and Zeus jumped up, following me into the house. All the furniture I didn't like had been taken away, but I was too damn lazy to pick out anything new. I'd donated damn near every piece that had come from Alaska. It just hadn't fit here. It was too much...Avery. I'd kept the bed, though. I couldn't bring myself to get rid of the one place I'd slept next to her, made love to her.

Maybe I should have told Bash that I wanted a different house, one she hadn't been in. He'd already been pissed at me for insisting on paying him for this one. Not that I cared. I wasn't going to live in a house that another man paid for—I didn't care if he called it a signing bonus or not. Maybe another house would have been better. One where I didn't see her smiling, crying out in pleasure, or picture her arching underneath me.

One where I didn't see her standing in my kitchen.

My heart stopped beating, my breath faltered, and the only muscle I moved were my eyelids, trying to blink away the vision of Avery standing at my stove, making breakfast.

Hell, I would have thought she was a mirage, if not for the smell of bacon and Zeus's excited yipping. Damn, that dog turned into a pitiful puppy when she was around...just like his owner.

"Hi," she said softly, the island between us.

"Hi."

She licked her lips nervously, her hair a wild tumble around her shoulders that I was desperate to slide my hands through. "So, I used my key."

"Finally. It only took me moving three thousand miles away to get you to do that." My feet were frozen. No matter how much I wanted to move, to get just the slightest bit closer to her, they wouldn't comply.

She forced a smile, and it was the most beautiful damn thing I'd seen since she'd smiled here six weeks ago. "I'm a little slow to act sometimes."

"Snails are faster," I agreed.

"I'm here," she said softly, her nervousness showing in the way she twisted the spatula in her hand.

"I've noticed," I said. *Why?* For the first time, I was scared to ask a damn question, scared that this was just a visit. Scared that all she wanted was my friendship when I loved her so much that I ached with it.

She swallowed, taking the rest of the bacon out of the pan and then moving it off the heat. "I thought maybe I was too late," she said, looking up at me as she came around the island in a pale blue sundress that matched her eyes to a T. "I wondered if you'd moved on. It's not like you're hard to look at," she muttered.

My forehead puckered, trying to figure out what the hell to say to her that wouldn't send her running back to Alaska.

"I had Harper drop me off. She has Adeline at the school right now, picking up enrollment papers."

My heart slammed to a beat again, life rushing through my veins. She was moving here. She'd brought Adeline.

She was staying.

"And when we pulled up, I was terrified that I'd find some other woman here, you know? Because I was so fucking stupid to let you go."

I stepped forward, and she put her hand out, taking a step back and shaking her head. "No. I told you once, I can't think when you touch me."

Every muscle in my body strained, demanding I reach for her, but locked down every one of them.

"But then I got out of the car and saw the flower beds," she whispered. Then she smiled so brightly that her entire face lit up. "And I saw the swing you put on the front porch, and I knew."

"Knew what?" I asked her, needing to hear the words.

"I knew that you hadn't moved on. That this was still *our* house, even if I'd pushed you away. I knew that you still loved me."

I almost laughed. Almost. "I've loved you for seven years. It would take a hell of a lot longer than five weeks to stop. It would take about seven eternities."

Her breasts rose and fell quickly as she struggled for control. "Thank God," she said as her voice broke. "Because I'm so in love with you that I don't know what I'd do if you ever stopped loving me."

Three steps and she was in my arms, my mouth fused to hers. The kiss was desperate, hungry, with an edge to it that I hadn't intended, but it was there all the same. I picked her up, and she wrapped those legs around me, her bare feet digging into my back as I carried her to the counter and set her ass on it.

"I missed you so fucking much," I told her in between kisses down her neck, the tops of breasts that peeked just above the fabric.

"River," she moaned, her hands tight in my hair, threading through where I had it pulled back. I'd never heard a more beautiful sound. "I can't think."

"Good," I told her, stroking my hand up her dress, caressing her thigh. "I let you think too much and look where that got us. From now on no head, just heart."

Her hand covered my heart. "What does yours tell you?"

I smiled, happiness bursting through me in ways I never thought would happen again. "That I'm going to love you until the day I die."

"Good," she said. "Now you'd better be quick. You've got maybe an hour before Addy is back."

"Welcome to life with a kid." I laughed, kissing her as my fingers slipped under her panties. "I haven't showered," I told her.

"I could not care less," she said, ripping my shirt over my head, then gasping as I parted her and ran my fingers from her slick entrance to her clit. "Just don't stop."

"There's no chance of that," I promised. "You're all I've thought about since I left Alaska." I stripped her panties off her and dropped my shorts to the ground, pulling her to the edge of the counter, my mind focused on getting inside her, fucking her until she couldn't ever think about walking away from me again, and then making love to her until she agreed to marry me. "Shit. Condoms are upstairs."

"I'm on birth control," she said, her voice breathless as she brought her mouth back to mine. "Now, River."

Raising her dress to her waist, I nudged her entrance with my dick and then thrust home.

Holy. Shit.

"I didn't imagine it," I said into her mouth between kisses. "We really are this good together."

She rocked her hips against me, her feet digging into my ass for leverage. I groaned and gave up trying to talk. I used my body to tell her everything I needed to say. Every thrust was my vow of love, every kiss my plea that she never leave me again.

Every gasp from her lips told me how much she'd missed me. Every rake of her nails told me she was as desperate for this as I was.

I grasped her hips and pulled her closer, changing our angle to hit her where I knew it would make her writhe.

"Yes, River. Yes." She chanted my name as I thumbed her clit, kissing her deeply, stroking her mouth with my tongue the same way I moved within her.

She was molten, pouring over me, setting me on fire as I thrust again and again, never giving her a chance to catch her breath.

She tightened around me, her cries growing louder, her breath catching and then holding as she came apart in my arms, arching against me. I was helpless against her, my orgasm ripping through me, shredding everything I was and rebuilding me as nothing more than Avery's man.

It was perfection.

She was perfection.

Our breathing was ragged as she stroked my hair, my lips pressed to her neck. "Wow," she said, reminding me of the first time she'd seen our house.

"Is that all you can say?" I asked her with a laugh.

"Do you have something better?" she asked with a grin as I pulled back to look in her eyes. She was so beautiful, her lips swollen from my kisses, her hair wild from my hands.

"I do."

She arched a delicate eyebrow at me.

"Welcome home, Avery."

EPILOGUE

Avery
Two years later

"$\mathcal{M}$idnight. Do you understand me?" River's voice was low and menacing.

"Y-y-yes, sir," the boy said as he stood in our entry hall.

"I don't care if it's homecoming. I don't care if you think you're getting lucky tonight. You touch her in any way she doesn't expressly ask for and they will never find your body."

The kid paled, and I did my best not to sputter in laughter as I watched my husband from the stairs. "Yes, sir," he said a little stronger now.

"Do you have condoms?"

"W-what?" the kid asked.

"Do you?" River barked.

"No, sir?" The kid panicked, looking back and forth like there was someone who might save him.

"Is that because you don't believe in safe sex, or because you are well aware that you won't be getting anywhere near her tonight?" River snapped.

"I...uh...I do believe in safe sex, I just haven't had any yet," the kid squeaked.

"Yet?" River barked.

"I'm not planning on starting tonight, sir!"

"Good answer. Midnight, or I come looking for you. I grew up here. I know all the spots, and I know exactly where your parents live. Do you understand me?"

"I do, sir." The kid managed to stand upright, which I knew got him a little more respect in River's eyes.

"Okay. As long as we understand each other, Devin."

"We do," the kid said.

"Is he done scaring him yet?" Addy asked, coming down the stairs in a silver, knee-length homecoming dress that made my little sister look like an angel.

"I think so. Maybe you should save him," I suggested.

"Did you get enough pictures?"

I thought of the three dozen or so on my camera. "I think so. I sent a couple to Dad already, and he said you look gorgeous. Did you find your purse?"

"I did." She hugged me. "Thank you."

"I love you. Be safe. Call me if you need anything, do you understand?"

"I do," she said.

Then she walked over to her date, kissing River's cheek first. "I'll be home by midnight, I promise."

"Uh huh," he muttered. "You're more likely to break the curfew than he is."

"Yeah, yeah. Love you," she told him before they headed out to the dance.

I came up behind River as he watched from the front bay window. "He opened her door," he said with approval.

Once they were out of the driveway, he pulled me into his arms. "She's going to be the death of me. I swear."

"You're good at this dad thing," I told River, reveling in the feel of him. A year of marriage and I still hadn't tired of this. Longest honeymoon period ever.

"You think?"

"I do. And I'm glad."

"Oh, are you?" he asked.

"Yeah, considering you'll get to do it from the beginning in about seven months." My teeth dug into my lower lip as I watched his every reaction.

He blinked down at me. "For real?" he whispered.

"Confirmed with the doc this morning," I told him, tears prickling my eyes.

Sheer wonder filled his eyes. "A baby."

"Our baby," I confirmed.

He kissed me deep, his hand protectively covering my belly. "Amazing. Just…perfect."

I sighed, leaning into his kiss. This was the kind of happiness I'd never dreamed of having, and yet here it was in overflowing abundance, filling every nook and cranny of my heart until I thought I'd burst.

His eyes flickered to the window and back to me. "Oh, God. What if it's a girl?"

I laughed. "Would that be so bad?"

"I know you Claire girls. I'm going to need another gun."

"Yeah, well, I can't wait to see how much trouble a Maldonado girl will be."

He paled. "Maybe two guns."

He kissed me again, and I sank into him, losing myself in his love and the promise that forever gave us.

Moving here, choosing a life with River, it hadn't just set me free.

It had brought me home.

The End

ALSO BY REBECCA YARROS

The Last Letter
Great and Precious Things
The Things We Leave Unfinished

Flight & Glory Series
Full Measures
Eyes Turned Skyward
Beyond What Is Given
Hallowed Ground
The Reality of Everything

The Renegades Series
Wilder
Nova
Rebel

Legacy Series
Point of Origin
Ignite

Written with Jay Crownover
Girl in Luv
Boy in Luv

Hush Notes Series
Muses & Melodies

ABOUT THE AUTHOR

Rebecca Yarros is the *Wall Street Journal* and *USA Today* bestselling author of over fifteen novels, and is also the recipient of the Colorado Romance Writer's Award of Excellence for *Eyes Turned Skyward* from her *Flight and Glory* series.

Rebecca loves military heroes and has been blissfully married to hers for twenty years. When she's not writing, you can find her at the hockey rink or sneaking in some guitar time while guzzling coffee. She and her family live in Colorado.

Having fostered then adopted their youngest daughter who is nonverbal and on the autism spectrum, Rebecca is passionate about helping children in the foster system through her nonprofit, One October, which she co-founded with her husband in 2019. To learn more about their mission to better the lives of kids in foster care, visit www.oneoctober.org.

To catch up on Rebecca's latest releases, including *The Things We Leave Unfinished*, visit www.RebeccaYarros.com.

Made in the USA
Middletown, DE
24 August 2024

59593033R00089